Cowboy Finding Love

COMING HOME TO NORTH DAKOTA
BOOK FOUR

JESSIE GUSSMAN

This is a work of fiction. Similarities to real people, places, or events are entirely coincidental. Copyright © 2022 by Jessie Gussman.

Written by Jessie Gussman.

All rights reserved.

No portion of this book may be reproduced in any form without written permission from the publisher or author, except as permitted by U.S. copyright law.

Contents

Acknowledgments	v
Chapter 1	1
Chapter 2	7
Chapter 3	13
Chapter 4	19
Chapter 5	27
Chapter 6	32
Chapter 7	38
Chapter 8	44
Chapter 9	46
Chapter 10	49
Chapter 11	56
Chapter 12	62
Chapter 13	65
Chapter 14	71
Chapter 15	78
Chapter 16	83
Chapter 17	86
Chapter 18	92
Chapter 19	101
Chapter 20	109
Chapter 21	119
Epilogue	127
Sneak Peek of Cowboy Dreaming Alone	131
A Gift from Jessie	137
Escape to more faith-filled romance series by Jessie Gussman!	139

Acknowledgments

Cover art by Julia Gussman
Editing by Heather Hayden
Narration by Jay Dyess
Author Services by CE Author Assistant

∽

Listen to the unabridged audio for FREE performed by Jay Dyess on the Say with Jay channel on YouTube. Get early access to all of Jay's recordings and listen to Jessie's books before they're available to the general public, plus get daily Bible readings by Jay and bonus scenes by becoming a Say with Jay channel member.

Chapter One

Communication, understanding, picking your battles, and never going to bed angry.
- Sharon Marks from the United States

"It's the Porsche again."

Gladys LeFrak wiggled her fingers—once—at the white handkerchief that weaved out of the cracked driver's side window of the bright red car, waving her own handkerchief from the equally tiny crack in her equally darkly tinted window.

She had no idea if the other driver was even a man or woman.

"They hug the yellow line," Silas Powers reminded her from his position in the passenger seat in a deep, rumbling voice.

His tone always calmed her. Or maybe it was just his personality. Calm. Not "cool."

He didn't strut around, and he was more quiet than any man she knew, but there was just something about him that grounded her.

She'd attempted to race one night without him. Something she would never do again.

"Got it," she said as she pulled her Lexus around beside the Porsche, which was slowly inching forward.

The two-lane North Dakota road stretched out, straight and flat, into the dark distance.

No other cars in sight at one o'clock in the morning. All of her neighbors in the sleepy little town of Sweet Water and surrounding area were sound asleep in their beds.

Nice people. Salt-of-the-earth people, but not the kind of people who stayed out past nine o'clock.

For goodness' sake, even the C-Store in Sweet Water closed at nine. Sometimes when there were no customers, it closed earlier.

The car beside her eased forward in the left lane. She eased up beside it in the right. Although being on the left added just a touch of danger, she would have preferred that position. Having the other car right beside her messed with her mind just a little. It was the optical illusion of it being so much closer than it was when she saw it on the passenger side.

"You have more under your hood than they do. You've got this." Silas's voice broke through the silence of her car.

The thumping of the other car's bass vibrated through their vehicle, the only thing disturbing their quietness. She preferred to race in silence.

On the way home, she'd want the windows down, the radio up.

If Silas had a preference, he'd never said.

The other car inched forward, and she gave it a slight lead while not allowing it to get too far ahead.

Silas was right. She'd beaten this Porsche before, but she couldn't come back from too big of a deficit. She needed to have her reflexes honed.

"Maybe they've done something since the last time we raced."

"That was just last Friday. It would have had to have been something quick and easy. Not enough time to give them more than what you've got."

His words, or maybe just his voice, stilled some of the cramping in her chest, although her heart still beat hard.

She loved the adrenaline surge. Lived for it.

And when the other car smashed the pedal to the floor, waiting a heartbeat or two before releasing the break, squealing the tires and laying a long track of rubber, she was ready.

Her own rubber trail was just as long, and she inched ahead of the Porsche before they covered a quarter of a mile.

She had this, as long as no vehicles came from the other direction.

She'd raced the same Porsche at least seven times, and the one time they met a car, the Porsche hadn't swerved or slowed down.

It was the only time it had beaten Gladys, since she hadn't been able to get within three hundred yards of the oncoming car before she pulled up off the gas and let the Porsche fly by. It had pulled into the right lane just in time, and by the time the car in the left lane had passed Gladys, she was down to a respectable eighty miles per hour.

Right now, the speedometer was tacked out at hundred fifty.

She was probably going much closer to two hundred mph.

But her car handled like a dream. No vibration in the steering wheel, and it hugged the road tightly.

"Dog."

Silas's voice cut through the silence a millisecond before she saw the prairie dog on the road.

Her side.

The Porsche never slowed, but immediately Gladys's foot lifted up from the accelerator, so she was probably only going hundred sixty or so when she hit it.

Just a glancing blow, but it was enough to make her lose control.

"You've got this." Silas's voice came out, comforting her and giving her confidence as the car skidded sideways. She steered into the skid before the rear end fishtailed, and she yanked the steering wheel the other way.

This skid wasn't quite as deep, and she might have been able to straighten out as she accelerated out of it, except the back left tire dropped off the pavement and onto the berm. It must have been a soft spot, because it caught the car, causing it to become airborne and flip.

Later, Gladys assumed that part, and Silas agreed. But she couldn't describe what happened next, other than hearing Silas's voice say, "Keep fighting. You've got it."

Otherwise, she couldn't have said what she did or what happened. All she knew was that the next concrete memory was of them sitting in the right-hand lane, facing in the proper direction, stopped. Four wheels down.

"Impressive," Silas's voice came again.

Her hands gripped the steering wheel, and she sat panting.

They could have died and almost did, and he was complimenting her driving. Like they had just taken a turn around the block.

"I think God had a hold of the wheel. I can't take credit for that."

"Normally I might argue with you, but I think you're right," he said, looking over at her.

She turned her head slowly, shaking her head at the grin on his face.

"People would never know to look at us that you're more addicted to danger than I am," she said with affection.

He grinned, lifting one side of his face in that familiar half smile that was his trademark. For her anyway.

Normally he was serious and quiet and let his actions do his talking, but that grin, and his encouragement, had become something she looked forward to.

"Thanks for staying calm. I know I've mentioned this before, but you help me stay grounded and focused."

"Need to have a purpose for sitting over here."

She smiled a little but wasn't sure exactly whether there might be some hidden meaning in those words.

He'd never asked to drive; she'd never offered, either.

He couldn't afford a car like this, not on a mechanic's salary, but he hadn't ever expressed any interest in owning one, not even a statement that could be interpreted that way.

"Now that I've calmed down a little, it makes me mad that Porsche has beaten me twice now. But both times because of external issues."

"I think that makes you a smarter driver. Sometimes, you need to know when to give up so you can walk away alive."

She grunted, nodding a little. Maybe she didn't care whether she walked away alive. She wasn't afraid, although she had been tonight, maybe not afraid exactly just...just overdosing on the adrenaline that a person gets when they know death is staring them in the face.

It wasn't a fear exactly.

"I guess I don't care if I die," she said, peeling her fingers from the steering wheel. It was true. What was there to live for?

She could do anything she wanted to and had. She'd gone to college, gotten her counseling degree. She'd just finished a master's program and had that diploma, too. But she wasn't sure where she wanted to go now.

The opportunities were greater back when she lived in California. She still had an apartment there but had been staying more and more with her parents because...well, she wasn't sure why.

Their dad had moved to North Dakota because of his business with the oil and needing to be on-site, and her mom, well, she hadn't wanted to move but had gone with her father.

Most of the time, Gladys figured her mom had moved because she was afraid if she wasn't around to babysit her dad, he'd leave her for someone younger and better looking.

He probably would, too. Her dad always seemed like a player to her. At least when she got old enough to know what a player was.

So she'd become one, too. It hadn't been satisfying, but it had given her something to do.

When her dad left California, it had been culture shock to land in North Dakota, and she happened to stop at Silas's family's garage to get a flat tire changed, which they hadn't been able to do, but Silas had just been going on his lunch break, and he'd taken it to drive her to Rockerton and pick her up one.

That had been two years ago, and that had been the beginning of their... was it a partnership?

She wasn't sure. But she'd been casually racing at night, just Silas and her, just for fun.

It had slowly grown into what she'd done tonight. Met up with someone, seemingly randomly, but the same spot she always waited at 1 AM on Friday night, and someone was always there.

Still, there wasn't really anything left for her to do or experience, other than marriage, and she wasn't really interested in that.

Except she kind of had to be. If she wanted to inherit her fortune that had been left to her from her grandmother.

If she didn't marry...she wouldn't inherit her fortune.

Gladys snorted.

"You okay?" Silas asked in the silence of the car.

She realized she'd never moved. Just been sitting there thinking.

"What's the point of life?" she asked, turning her head.

Silas's concerned look didn't ease.

He knew a ton about cars and had learned more since their association. After all, he'd told her over and over that his expertise was with diesel repair, which was different than gasoline engines.

Completely different.

But North Dakota was a big state, though sparsely populated, and lots of people did more than one thing, so Silas had learned about gasoline engines.

And he'd built her what she had.

In the process, she had grown to respect him. He had a lot of wisdom, and he was thoughtful and deliberate about what he did. He didn't make rash decisions, but he enjoyed speed just as much as she did, because he was always ready at 12:45 on Friday night when she picked him up at his house.

"Are you looking for a reason to live? Or are you asking what the point of your life is?"

"Aren't they one and the same?" she asked, looking back out the windshield, feeling stupid for having said it. It wasn't like they hadn't talked about deep things before, because they had, but they had never been personal.

She put on a tough persona to the world, and most of the time, she kept that facade for Silas's benefit as well. She didn't want to appear weak in front of him, of all people. Since he was probably the person she respected most in the world.

He'd earned it. Because with Silas, what a person saw was what a person got.

He didn't put on a big show, not like she was used to. Not just with her family, her parents especially, but with her friends as well. They were all busy trying to look sophisticated and cool and fit in with the crowd. Whatever that was, whatever they had to change about their outer shell in order to cover what they really were and be like everyone else.

Silas was what he was, and he seemed to be very content with that.

"I don't think so. A reason to live might be because you don't want to hurt your family by your death. Or you have things you want to accomplish and aren't ready to go until you've done your best with them. The point of your life is the meaning. Why you're here."

"And why is that?" she asked, almost bitterly.

Nothing she did made a difference. She'd never done one thing for her life to have a point. She wasn't supposed to. She was just supposed to look good and be an accessory, and while she certainly could apply for a position to use her degree, all she could see were endless lines of rich people coming to her complaining about problems that didn't really matter while she sat and listened and asked them how they felt about that and listened some more, then gave them advice that they both knew they weren't going to listen to and took their money.

She'd been to enough counseling sessions herself to know how it worked.

She'd had some vague notion of helping people when she'd gone for her degree, but that had evaporated quickly as she'd listened to her professors and fellow students.

It was about the money. It was always about the money.

Chapter Two

Praying together.
- Ginni Selby from Delta, CO

"God made you so that you can bring glory to Him and point others to Christ," Silas finally said. It was the same tone he always used, but as attuned to him as she was, she could sense the slight tightening of his muscles, tell he had tensed.

He'd talked about God a few times before. That wasn't what their conversations were always about, but a few times. He'd discussed Jesus as well, and while Gladys didn't always understand why everything had to be so bloody and difficult, she did understand that a God who made everything could make His own rules.

"Do you think we should get out and look to see if the car is okay?" she asked.

"It didn't touch anything, so as long as the tires are fine, we should be good. I'll look." He moved to unbuckle his seat belt and opened his door.

Funny, as much of a daredevil as she was, and as much as he seemed unafraid to do whatever she did, they both always wore their belts. Today was the first day that she was actually happy about that.

Before, she hadn't really thought about it. It was just what they were programmed to do.

Opening her door, she got out. The road was completely deserted in either direction, and the wind, which seldom stopped in North Dakota, blew almost directly from the west.

That was another thing she had to get used to when moving to North Dakota. Everyone out here talked about actual physical directions. North, south, east, west. She could understand why, since everything was flat and it was easy to tell which direction a person was facing.

"You know," she said to him when they met at the back of her car, which did not have a scratch on it, and the tires looked perfect, too. "If I hadn't already decided that you were right about there being a God, having something like that happen to me would have convinced me."

His lip tilted up. "And I think that you can assume, because God made sure that you landed rubber side down, with the paint intact, that He probably needs you for something and wants you down here on earth to do whatever it is."

"What in the world could He possibly want from me?"

Silas lifted his shoulder.

"You know I'm going to have to choose a man and get married." She grunted. "Which is the stupidest thing I've ever heard of. Barbaric almost."

"For someone to have to get married to inherit their inheritance?" He looked around at her.

"For a woman to have to get married. Why is it always women?"

"You don't have brothers. Maybe she would have made a stipulation for them, too."

"Probably not," Gladys said, but Silas was right. Her gram was eccentric that way and probably would have done the same thing if she had brothers. But it was just her and her sister. Which meant the fortune was just theirs, too. As long as they married by the time they were twenty-five.

"Maybe that's what has me so depressed. That's pretty much all my mom says to me every time she sees me. And Saturday night, they have not one but two people with Ivy League educations coming for supper. I am required to attend," she said in her snobby rich girl voice. Letting him know exactly how badly she wanted to not attend.

He didn't move, didn't say anything, just stared down at her, his lips pressed together. His gaze dark and unreadable.

"I could use a little sympathy here?" she finally said. Then rolled her eyes, turned on her toes, and walked to her car door.

Often, Silas would open her door for her. It was an old-fashioned gesture that made her smile. But she didn't slow down or turn to see if he would do it this time. She was a little annoyed.

He was just like everyone else in that area. Didn't understand that having money wasn't the easy life everyone thought it was. It came with a lot more requirements, a lot more restrictions, a lot more things that she could and couldn't do because people were watching and might think poorly of her family, or because she was supposed to be some kind of example. But mostly because the families of rich men were watching, and rich men themselves were watching, and her mother wanted her to make a good match.

As she often said, she didn't want Gladys to end up the wife of a common laborer.

Like that was a fate worse than death.

She was already sitting in her seat with her seat belt on when Silas's door opened, and he slid in, graceful as always, reminding her of a tiger, the smooth movements, the unleashed aggression, the hint of power, the eye of a hunter.

Before he had his seat belt snapped, she had put the car back in gear and did a U-turn right there on the road.

The Porsche had never come back. Not to check, not to see what happened.

Sometimes she wondered about the people she raced, but mostly she didn't care. Maybe he lived in a town west of Sweet Water, maybe he found another way home, taking care not to meet her. She did know she'd never seen that Porsche, or any of the other cars she raced, around Sweet Water.

They'd driven for a while, through Sweet Water and out the other side, and Silas still hadn't said a word.

One thing she liked about him was that he didn't cater to her. When she was angry or annoyed with him, he didn't act like he needed to crawl around on his hands and knees trying to make her happy with him again.

He seemed to understand that sometimes she just needed to get upset and get over it.

And he gave her that space.

Turning right out of Sweet Water, she headed toward the small house he'd bought less than a year ago. It wasn't far from his family's garage but enough distance away that it gave him some privacy and a place to come to in the evenings.

A place to work on her car where no one could see it.

"Sorry I snapped at you," she finally said.

Silas was the best friend she had. Maybe he wasn't the closest friend, but he was loyal and dependable, and she could call him anytime about anything and know with certainty that he would do everything in his power to help her.

A friend like that was invaluable.

"Your car, I can help you with. Your inheritance and the hoops you have to jump through in order to get it, I can't."

"I know. It's not like I have to stay married in order to get it. I think there's like a six-month contract or something. So I don't have to tie myself down for the rest of my life. But...I just hate the thought."

"If you make vows, you have to keep them."

Often, when Silas disagreed with her, he asked her questions which made her think. So this was unusual—him announcing that something had to be done.

She opened her mouth as the gravel crunched under the car as she turned in his driveway. "But I'd be just doing it so I get the money. I wouldn't really mean them."

"Then you can't say them."

"You're making this more complicated than it needs to be."

"Marriage is uncomplicated. Simple. You make vows, you keep them."

Her lip pulled back as she searched his face.

That was one of his things—making things simple and right.

It was something a person should do, and she knew it. Keep their word. Don't say things they don't mean. Don't make promises they couldn't keep. Everyone knew that. Silas was more concerned about that than most, because of his walk with his God.

Going with her was the only thing she could think of that might even stretch the boundaries Silas had made for himself, since technically they were braking the law by speeding, although at night in North Dakota when there was no one else on the roads and the roads were straight as they could be, they weren't likely to hurt anyone, and it didn't bother her at all.

She supposed, if it weren't for her, Silas wouldn't be doing it.

"Then what do you suggest I do? Just give up the money?"

"Find a man you can say those vows to and mean them. Keep them." He looked out the window, his hand on the door latch. "Or yeah. Give up the money. It's not worth lying about."

She paused with her hand on the latch. "But it's millions of dollars!"

He leaned forward as though he were going to stand, but then he stilled. "But your reputation. Your word. Your honor. All of that is more important and worth more than millions of dollars. Billions of dollars. You can't buy it. You have to live it."

"I turn twenty-five this fall. I don't have much time, not just to find a man that I want to say those vows to and mean them but to convince him to marry me. So I have to think of something else. I don't have a choice."

Silas pushed the door open, moving to get out. Normally, he'd talk as long as she wanted to—he was as unhurried as a summer day—but he almost seemed agitated tonight, and she wasn't sure why. Maybe it was the almost accident.

"I guess it's easy for me to say 'give up the money,' since I've never had any, and I feel like it's not that hard to live without it. But I can see why it might be difficult for you."

She nodded. She didn't want to live with no money.

"But the Bible says it's easier for a camel to go through the eye of a needle than it is for a rich man to enter into the kingdom of heaven. I'm not sure I know exactly what that means, but I guess I can kinda understand that maybe one of the ideas is that it's wrong to sacrifice our integrity to get our inheritance."

He wasn't attacking her; she wouldn't take it that way at all. If there was one thing she was sure about, it was that Silas was on her side. He'd never shown any inclination of anything else.

"Well, are you hiring? Because I'm gonna need to get a job."

One side of his mouth lifted up. "You and I both know you weren't made to work in a garage. As much as you love fast cars, this is just a phase. Maybe letting loose a little after all the studying you did for your degrees." He paused. "Live up to your potential. Embrace it. Make your life count. You wanted to know what the point was, make a point, if you can't find one. Ask God what He wants from you. Then do it."

By that time, both sides of his mouth were smiling, and his teeth flashed in the darkness as he leaned back.

"Come around anytime. You know you're welcome." He backed out and slammed the door shut.

That was new. He'd never ended one of their evenings together with an invitation to come back. She just always had.

Normally, she pulled away, parking her Porsche by the garage and swapping out for the Lexus she normally drove, before he made it into the house, but tonight she sat and watched as he walked up the steps to the porch. Interestingly, he didn't open the door but turned, then leaned against the porch post, his arms crossed over his chest, as though he were waiting for her to pull out before he went in.

It was endearing about him, the values and morals and character that made up his personality, that made him interesting to her. Attractive.

He was a man she would marry in three months, without thinking twice about it. He would do right by her, even if it hurt him. He was that kind of man.

You've not been that kind of woman.

Ouch. The voice in her head was right. She hadn't been that kind of woman. Not the kind of woman who would do right for others even if it hurt herself.

The kind of woman that people could depend on, blindly, because they knew she'd do what she said she was going to.

How could she admire him so much and want to be friends with him, maybe even taking advantage of his friendship, because she didn't return it? Didn't return anything that he did.

Thinking about it that way, she didn't like what she saw in herself, and rather than asking about the point of life, she wondered what she needed to do in order to fix it.

Chapter Three

Trust always and laughter and smiles every day even in the worst times.
- Carole Palmer from Richardton, North Dakota

Silas hit the brakes, and his pickup came to a stop. He slipped it into reverse.

He'd worked late at the garage, and the sun had just set, leaving the North Dakota plains bathed in a dying orange glow.

He was pretty sure the furry little body he'd just seen along the road was not a prairie dog.

Watching carefully in his side mirrors, just in case whatever it was decided to come out onto the road, he backed up, ready to brake at the first sign of movement.

He hadn't been going fast, so he didn't need to back up far and stopped where he thought he'd seen it.

There was nothing there, but he could see the tall grass on the side of the road waving.

With the transmission in neutral, he put on the parking brake and hopped out. He could have sworn it was a puppy. Looked like a little shaggy ball of fur, maybe a terrier mix, but he hadn't gotten a good look. Especially with the sun going down.

Another wave rippled through the tall grass. The breeze felt good after the heat of the day, and Silas took a minute to lift his head, putting it in the wind and allowing it to blow across his skin.

Breathing deeply, he felt contentment clear down to his soul.

Contentment in his life, contentment that he was where he was supposed to be, contentment that God had a plan for him, and he was living it.

At least, that was most of what he felt.

Part of him was a little irritated that he was so attracted to a woman who was so wrong for him.

It was something he'd been praying about, and he figured he probably had to take some steps on his own to move away from her so he wouldn't be as tempted.

He studied the grass, walking slowly, not wanting to scare whatever it was. He supposed it was possible for it to be a wolf pup, but he hadn't seen the body of the mother along the road, and it just seemed a bit little to be out of the den anyway. Not that he knew that much about wolves. Just knew he heard them occasionally at night, sometimes could relate to the howling.

A small whine lifted above the breeze and the rustle of the grass.

"Hey, little guy. It's not safe for you to be here along the road," he said, talking gently, hoping the sound of his voice would reassure the pup.

There weren't a whole lot of animal shelters in North Dakota, and sadly, it wasn't uncommon for people to dump unwanted animals along the edge of the road.

If that's what happened, Silas would guess he was dealing with a little female. They were more expensive to fix.

Movement caught his eye, and he saw two little floppy ears and two bright eyes shining out of the grass stems.

A little lower and there was a wet shiny nose. Altogether, the face looked sad yet hopeful.

"You want to come on out? I'll take you home and give you a little something to eat. Maybe we can find somebody who's missing you."

It was possible the little lady had run away, but as small as she was, and as far as they were away from any houses, he highly doubted it.

He hunkered down on his haunches and held a hand out.

It took a couple minutes, but the little pup crept forward slowly. Stopping, sniffing, and whining. Silas held still, talking softly, holding his hand out, but not moving.

Thankfully no cars came, since he hadn't bothered to pull his pickup off the road. The road wasn't well used, and it was straight as a plumb line, so any car would be able to see his truck sitting there well before they came upon it.

Thoughts of the night before, and Gladys's near miss, shot through his head.

He'd been a lot more scared than he let on, but he'd figured out long ago that his calmness gave Gladys courage.

He also figured out she was a pretty amazing woman. But she wasn't a happy one.

Last night had been the first time that she'd given him a glimpse of the emptiness she felt.

He'd seen it before. She wasn't happy, despite having everything her heart could desire. Wasn't happy because she didn't have a purpose, and she was living for herself, no one else.

He shook his head. Finding it funny that he'd be attracted to someone like that, but it was true.

The first time she walked into the shop, he'd pretty much been lost. Even knowing she was more self-centered than someone he should be interested in, he allowed their friendship to grow and had never turned her down when she'd invited him to go with her.

A relationship between a rich girl and a poor boy wasn't quite as taboo as it had been years ago, socially anyway.

But she just saw him as a friend. Maybe at some point, he crossed the line from being just a friend to being a good friend, but it wasn't hard for him to see that she would never want more with him.

"Come on. Just another couple of steps and I'll scratch your ears."

The pup was completely out on the blacktop now and was cautiously sniffing.

"You want your mom, don't you?" he asked, knowing that feeling. Wanting his mom. Wasn't nearly as bad now as it had been when he was younger. He supposed a person never outgrew their longing for their mother. Maybe it just changed over time as they became an adult. Wanting her for comfort and security turned into wanting her more just because it would be nice to have someone older and wiser who could give him advice and would love him no matter what he did.

Give him advice on what to do when he couldn't get his mind off a girl that was completely wrong for him.

Not that there weren't good qualities in Gladys, because there were plenty.

Being brave and willing to take chances could be incredible assets if funneled into the right place. Which, being that she currently used them to drag race her car at night, was definitely a misuse of her gifts, but they were still there.

She was also generous, and while her family was rich, and she wouldn't consider marrying someone like him, there was no snob about her.

The pup's cold nose touched his fingers. Silas froze, letting the little bundle sniff his hand. Maybe it smelled of the hoagie he'd had this evening with Flynn, who had worked late with him.

They had a truck torn down and needed to get it back on the road for the weekend. Flynn usually kept the books, and he was good at it, but he could also turn a wrench if he needed to. Because of the precision in his personality, when he picked up the wrench, he was good at what he did, it just wasn't something that was as interesting to him as crunching numbers and manipulating data points.

Soon enough, a warm tongue came out and dragged across his fingers. Now that she was out of the bushes, he could definitely see a little St. Bernard in her too. She was going to be a big dog, furry with a happy personality, from what he could tell.

Still, she couldn't be that old, because her little belly sagged beneath her, and her legs were wobbly.

He'd almost bet money that someone had tossed her out, and whoever had done it had probably pulled her away from her mom well before she should have been weaned. Maybe so their kids wouldn't fall in love with her since she was a sweetheart.

She allowed him to run his hands over her head and scratch her little ears. She whined, like she still thought maybe he could help her find her mom again.

"I hope you're big enough to at least lap milk, if not crunch on a little bit of dog food," he murmured.

He had a little bag left from when he had watched Dodge and Marigold's puppy when they'd gone on vacation. That would tide her over until morning when he could make it to the store. If she was able to eat. He wasn't sure how old dogs had to be before they could at least slurp up soggy dog food.

"How do you feel about coming home with me, girlfriend?" he said, wrapping his hand around her belly and noting that she didn't seem afraid.

He scooped her up and pulled her against his chest where she snuggled.

Maybe he just fell in love too easily, because at that moment, he figured he probably lost his heart to the little puppy, and although he knew he would try to find her owner, he was really hoping she was a stray he'd end up keeping.

Several hours later, Silas had finished going over Gladys's car, amazed again at what a miracle it had been that they hadn't been hurt at all.

It was almost as though God's hand had guided the car, gently flipping it over and setting it back down on its wheels.

Silas really couldn't think of any other explanation for why the car hadn't been totaled and they hadn't been killed.

There wasn't a scratch on it.

Even the tires seemed to be okay. He put it on the lift—something he'd installed in the garage not long after he bought the place—and checked and double-checked the undercarriage, giving particular attention to the wheels and axles.

It was completely unbelievable that the car didn't have a thing wrong with it. Not a thing.

He stood with his hands hanging loosely on the front bumper, his head hanging down, humbled by the grace that God gave.

He'd told Gladys that God must have a plan for her life, but he figured the Lord must have something in store for him as well, since there was just no physical explanation for why he wasn't currently dead.

A little snort, a groan, and then a long sigh cut through his thoughts.

He smiled at the little bundle over in the corner.

He'd grabbed some rags and even had a piece of foam that he'd thrown together for a little bed.

Once he got her to eat, which hadn't been hard, she'd been just fine.

The package he had from Dodge's pup said it was complete nutrition for dogs, so he didn't add any milk or eggs to it, although he'd been tempted to. It just hadn't seemed like enough to put a bunch of dry stuff in front of a little puppy and think it would help her grow.

He hadn't trusted the package, and had done a little searching on the Internet, and had come to the same conclusion.

When she'd been done eating, she had lapped a little at the water he'd set down in a bowl he'd made from cutting off an empty jug and rinsing it out. Then he'd held her some before she fell asleep in his arms, and he laid her down on the blankets.

She hadn't wanted to stay there, but he'd sat with her for a bit, until she'd fallen asleep and not noticed when he got up and walked back over to continue working.

He hated to do it, but tomorrow he'd have to stop in and see the Piece Makers, give them some of the pictures he'd taken, and ask them if they'd help him find out if she belonged to someone.

If anyone would know if there was a puppy missing in Sweet Water, it would be the Piece Makers.

Pulling a rag out of his pocket, he wiped his hands, intent on quitting for the night.

He jerked his head up at the sound of the door opening, It was after midnight, and he wasn't expecting visitors.

It could only be something bad. He'd barely thought that when Gladys walked in, her face ashen, her eyes frantically flying around until they landed on him.

"Silas!" she said, relief and fear and almost desperation lacing her tone.

He couldn't get "what happened?" out of his mouth before she strode across the floor and threw her arms around him.

Their relationship had never been a physical relationship, so he hesitated a minute from surprise.

Whatever had happened had really upset her. He could feel her shaking as he wrapped his own arms around her, unwilling to split hairs over exactly what their relationship was.

As big as her personality was, as much courage as she had, she felt small and almost delicate in his arms. Something he wasn't expecting.

Neither had he ever expected her to hold onto him, like she needed support.

He thought of her as self-sufficient, confident, and fearless.

Which made her clinging to him now all the more alarming.

There had never been any alcohol involved in anything that he'd ever done with her, but he still sniffed the air, wondering if that might be it.

All he smelled was something pleasant and a little wild, something that reminded him of courage and carefree attitude.

The scent he always associated with Gladys.

It was his favorite.

Her head tucked under his chin, and her hands held him tight. He wasn't sure how long they stood like that, with his fingers stroking her back and him trying to do what he always seemed to be able to for her, which was allow his quiet calmness to ease her mind and give her strength.

His prayer for Gladys, almost since he'd met her, ran through his head too.

Lord, she knows You. Draw her close and help her to turn to You.

Finally, the almost panicked grip of her arms loosened, and she sniffed.

He hadn't thought she'd been crying. He hadn't heard a sound anyway, but the sniff seemed telling.

She didn't raise her head but seemed to press closer to him.

"My parents were killed in a car accident on their way to the airport."

Chapter Four

Commitment to make it; both to your spouse and to God.
- Deborah McCoy

Silas's eyes widened. Gladys had lost both parents? And so suddenly.

"You know I wasn't exactly close with either of them, but it's still a shock. They...are...were...my parents."

"Of course. Wow."

He didn't know what else to say. *I'm so sorry for your loss* seemed so trite. It didn't begin to scratch the surface of what a person had to feel in a tragedy of this proportion.

"They were supposed to be going to a business meeting in The Cities. They were taking a red-eye because Dad had to finish up work today before he could leave."

Again, he felt like he needed words, but he didn't have any. Instead, he eased his hands over her back, slender but unfamiliar. It was hard to believe the woman in his arms tonight was the same one who had driven the car with him last night, fearlessly and almost arrogantly.

But maybe this was what she needed. Maybe it was what they both needed. A reminder that they might feel like they were in control of their lives, but they really weren't. That sometimes it seemed like they didn't need the Lord, but life was too hard to try to handle on their own.

"I need to tell Mabel." Her voice sounded rough, like it had been run over rocks. The anguish in it was clear.

"Yeah...there are probably a lot of other things you need to do too. If you need me beside you, you know I'll be there."

That was really all he could offer. Just his presence. His support. His... whatever it was he had that gave her what she needed.

She took a deep breath at his words, and his arms tightened, before she leaned back.

"I don't know what it is about you, but there is a calmness, an aura around you that makes whatever I'm going through easier. It gives me focus."

She looked down before her eyes, which were dry despite her sniff, met his. "I feel like I'm using you, because I never give anything back. I realized last night our relationship is very one-sided."

As always, he was unsure of what to say about that. He could hardly tell her that he just enjoyed being with her, maybe because of the little attraction between them, or because he just enjoyed watching her. So confident and carefree. Maybe because of the money she had grown up with, knowing she had every opportunity offered to man and could have whatever she wanted.

Or maybe confidence was just her natural personality. He wasn't sure, but he'd never met anyone like her, and from the moment he'd seen her, he wanted to spend as much time as he could with her.

Even if that meant drag racing after the sun went down.

Although, as he stood, his hands still on her back, he realized there'd always been a rightness there. The feeling that he was exactly where he was supposed to be. He felt it even stronger now. Like he was needed. Like the words he just said were the exact right ones.

He wasn't sure exactly what that meant, either for him or for Gladys, but he just knew that whatever she needed, he needed to be there for her.

"You can't do that. You have a job. You had a motor torn down. Your brothers are counting on you to fix it."

"And sometimes life gives us things which are unexpected. My brothers know that. My family knows that, and not one of them would begrudge me helping someone who's experiencing the tragedy that you are. Don't give it another thought."

Her eyes, so blue they were almost black, seemed to search his face, making sure he meant what he said, like there had ever been a time he hadn't.

He allowed his lips to curve up a little. "Has there ever been a time I've told you something I didn't mean?"

She slowly shook her head, a thoughtful look on her face like she was going back through the memories she had of them together and realizing that was completely true. He did not just spew out words.

"I was at home when I got the call about my parents. I called several friends in California. They'll be flying in, tomorrow and the next day." She hesitated, as though she didn't want him to be offended. "Until they get here, I appreciate being able to lean on you."

He nodded. He wasn't offended. He knew he wasn't in her class or her circle. It included people who lived lives he couldn't even imagine. And while that hurt in a way, he also understood it, even though he wouldn't be the same.

He valued loyalty and steadfast character. If he was someone's friend, he was their friend no matter what they did or who they were or where they went.

So he would be Gladys's friend as long as she wanted him.

"I'll be beside you as long as you want me," he said, stroking her hair as she tucked her head back under his chin and squeezed.

"Thank you," she said softly. "I don't even know what to do. I mean, I'm going to have to identify the bodies." Her voice broke a little on the last word, like she couldn't stand talking about her parents as bodies and not people.

"I'll be there," he said, although inside, he wasn't sure it was something he would be able to handle. He prayed for a little more strength, because he figured he was going to need it if he was going to have to look at dead bodies.

People did this all the time. Every day. If they could do it, he could do it too.

"And I'm going to have to meet with our accountant. Dad had one on payroll. I have no idea how to do anything with the business. I... I showed up when they asked me to, did what they said, and never put too much thought into it."

"That's fine. You're smart. Your parents did it. And you're their child. You can figure it out."

His words were confident, because he believed it. It was another thing he admired about Gladys. She was fearless, almost to the point of being arrogant, but she wasn't stupid. She made smart decisions and had a natural knack for putting information together in her head and coming out with the right choice no matter how much time she had to think.

For him, it usually took a little bit more time to process. He needed to roll the ideas over in his head, ponder them some, sleep on it even, before he came up with a choice that made sense.

"I'm glad you think so," she said.

He took her by her shoulders and pushed her away from him a little. As much as he didn't want her to let go, he felt like she needed to understand that he wasn't just saying it, but it was true.

He waited until her gaze lifted to meet his before he shook her shoulders just a little and said, "You can do it. You don't have to do it all tonight. Or tomorrow. Or the next day. Just focus on the task in front of you, do that, even if it's sleeping, which," he tilted his head a little, "that's probably the task that you have to do right now."

She lifted her brows in acknowledgment with one lip turned back. But she didn't say anything.

"Then God will give you the strength to do whatever it is He has laid out for you to do next and next. And God's given you me for now. And when your friends from LA come, you have them. It's not like you have to be strong and do this all on your own, and I think you've already figured that out."

"You're right. I have. I guess that's why I'm here. I know I can't do it on my own." She sighed. "But I'm not used to asking God for help. I've... I've often thought I don't even need it. It seems a little like I'm using Him, too, if I go to Him now when I'm having problems, when I haven't been around before when I didn't."

"Maybe that's why He had this happen. Because your parents' jobs on earth are done, and He wanted to draw you closer to Him." He paused, not wanting to scare her but deciding that Gladys was the kind of woman who rose to the challenge rather than sat around afraid. "Maybe He has a job for you to do, and He needs you to be closer to Him in order to do it. Maybe it's running your parents' company, or maybe it's something else."

It was funny, but he never even considered giving her advice that might lead her more toward him, even though that's what he wanted to do. Advice that might make her decide that being with him was a good choice. Which was...what he wanted if he really thought about it. His advice always had to be what he truly thought was best for the person he was talking to, not for himself.

Sometimes that was the hardest thing about giving advice—saying something that would almost guarantee that the things he wanted wouldn't happen.

But there was no way he could do otherwise—he had to say what he thought was best for her and not for himself.

"You mean something else other than dealing with my parents' deaths? God would heap something else on me?" she asked, almost as though she thought this was the only trial she should have to face at this point in her life.

"In my life, at least, it feels like sometimes God gives me trial after trial after trial before He gives me a break. Almost as though He wants to see how I'll handle it when I feel overwhelmed and unable to do anything for myself."

Her face scrunched up. "I can't imagine you feeling overwhelmed." The first semblance of a smile stole over her face. "I've never seen anyone with such an absolute calm about them."

"Maybe what you see on the outside isn't a great indication of what's going on on the inside."

His small smile matched hers, and he dropped his hands from her shoulders, rubbing them along her upper arms which were cold. He'd never touched her before, so maybe it was normal for her skin to be cold, but she just wore a T-shirt and jeans. Even though it was summer in North Dakota, the nights were still chilly, especially clear ones like this evening.

"Mabel was already in bed, sound asleep. I can't tell her tonight, and I guess I'll have to tell Kayla, our housekeeper. And... There's a million people I'm going to need to talk to tomorrow."

"All the better reason to get a good night's sleep tonight." He looked over at the corner where his new pup still slept soundly. "I can drive you home if you need me to."

She shivered. "I don't want to go home. I can't stand the thought of it. Walking into the dark and quiet house, knowing I have to make all the decisions from now on. I...I might have a postgrad degree, but I've never had this kind of responsibility before, and it feels like a ton of bricks on my chest. I can't breathe." She said the last on a puff of breath as she pushed against him again and hugged his waist.

His hands came up automatically, covering her back.

This wasn't something he would normally do; in fact, he couldn't even have imagined a situation like this before, but he found himself whispering over her head, "Come on in my house."

"Your house?" she asked, sounding surprised and relieved at the same time.

"Yeah. I was planning on sleeping on the couch anyway."

"You were going to sleep on the couch?" she asked after a moment's pause, as though she had needed to think about his words before she actually believed what he said since it sounded so odd.

"Yeah. I found a puppy alongside the road tonight. I figured I might need to get up and let her out a couple of times."

"A puppy? Where is it?" This time, she pulled back on her own, and he was grateful for the puppy. Wondering if maybe that had been the Lord's plan all along. Knowing there was going to be a tragedy tonight, and who wouldn't rather think about a puppy than death?

"She's over there in the corner. I haven't named her. You can if you want to, although I was kind of dragging my feet about it because I need to find out if she belongs to anyone before I can keep her for sure."

He didn't go into all the reasons that he figured she was probably an unwanted dump off, but just left it as it was.

"Oh, my goodness," Gladys said as she walked slowly over, kneeling down beside the puppy.

In all the time they'd spent together, all the hours they'd been at the garage, they'd talked about a variety of stuff, but never animals. Maybe it was a bit of a surprise to see Gladys enamored with the little dog who stretched and groaned as she rubbed her stomach.

"I always wanted a dog, but my parents said no. They didn't want the mess in the house, and I didn't see the point in getting a dog that had to be kept outside all the time."

She spoke without looking up, rubbing the pup. As she did, Silas walked slowly over, bending down on his haunches beside her.

"If she doesn't have a home with anyone else, she's yours if you want her." Silas didn't want to give the dog away. He'd already fallen in love with her himself, but if she would be a friend to Gladys, a loyal friend, through what was surely going to be a difficult time for her, he would happily let her go.

"I can't take your dog," she exclaimed.

"She's not mine. I mean, I still need to check around and make sure she doesn't belong to anyone. I understand if you don't want to keep her until we're sure she's yours to keep."

"I'd really like her. She seems like a sweetheart. But it might be best if she just stays here, because I don't know how crazy my life is going to get. Can I borrow her to snuggle with at least? And then can I wait and give you my decision after you check around to make sure she doesn't belong to anyone else?"

"That sounds reasonable."

The puppy stretched and climbed clumsily to her feet.

"I think we better take her outside. Usually when they wake up, they have to go."

"How do you know so much about dogs?"

"We had a couple when I was growing up, although they're harder to keep now that we're older and never know whether we'll be home or not."

He straightened up, and Gladys walked beside him to the door, the puppy following along behind.

He didn't bother shutting the lights off, because he needed to come back in and take the food and water to the house.

"That was an interesting makeshift water container," Gladys said, giving him a teasing glance before her eyes clouded, like she'd forgotten for a moment all the responsibilities that awaited her in the morning.

The puppy barely made it to the grass before she squatted. Silas eyed her for a second before his attention went back to Gladys.

Gladys hardly seemed like the kind of woman who was touchy-feely, but today was an exception, so he took another step and put his arm around her, pulling her to his side. She went willingly and laid her head on his shoulder.

"I forgot for a second, then I remembered, and then I felt guilty for forgetting. I should be crying right now. I should be hysterical. I should be—"

"Everyone grieves differently. And as a person, you're going to grieve differently for different people. Don't tell yourself how you 'should' be. You don't have to *be* any certain way."

"That's easy for you to say. People are going to look at me tomorrow, expecting me to behave in certain ways, and they're going to be upset and offended if I don't."

"You don't want to offend people by being unkind. You don't want to offend people by being rude or mean. But if you're offending people because you're not acting the way they think you should act, you can ignore those people, because they're just using their offendedness to try to manipulate you into doing and being who and what they want you to be and do. And they don't have that right."

Maybe he was being a little bossy or commanding, but Gladys already had enough on her plate; she didn't need to walk on eggshells because she wasn't acting or behaving or grieving the way everyone in her circles thought she ought to.

"They're using their offendedness to manipulate me," she said softly, as though rolling that over in her mind. "I've never considered that before, but you're right. People say they're offended, like it was something I had done, that the trespass was mine. But...that's not true. They're the ones who are looking at me and trying to make me behave the way they want me to."

"If it's not a moral behavior, then they have no right. Because you have every right to believe the way you want to, act the way you want to, and grieve the way you need to, and they are wrong to try to use their offense to manipulate you into doing things the way they want them done."

"That's why I always enjoy talking with you. You have a perspective that I don't. And you made me think."

"Maybe you'll feel like crying in the morning. You can do it then if you want to."

"I'm going to have too much stuff to do. I can't cry then. And I don't want to cry at all."

"Then don't. Or do. Whatever you want, your grief is yours."

She walked beside him back into the garage, his arm still around her. He went in long enough to shut the lights off and scoop the puppy and food up with his free hand. She was probably big enough to walk across the grass, but he didn't want to lose her in the dark.

They stepped out into the dark night, the door clicking closed behind them, a million stars shining overhead, and a soft breeze rustling the grass.

Tonight was so different than last night, even though the weather was the same, the sky the same, the breeze the same, and the grass just one day older. So much had changed.

Funny how life could shift in an instant.

He had thought that yesterday, then today, for Gladys at least, it had.

For him too, if Gladys was going to stay the night.

"You still want to stay?" he asked softly.

Chapter Five

Communication.
- Carolyn from Encino, Ca

Gladys lifted her eyes to Silas, wide in the moonlight, and he could see the fear and anxiety over the thought of going back home.

"If you don't mind?"

"Not at all."

She smiled, shifting around as she reached for the puppy.

He handed her over easily, and Gladys snuggled her down in her arms while Silas pulled her close again and guided her along the path to the house.

"I just have a small bed in my guest room. You can sleep there. Or—"

"Couldn't I sleep on the couch with you and the pup? I don't want to be alone."

"Of course," he answered immediately and kept walking even as he racked his brain for some verse, something that would tell him that what he was doing was wrong.

Maybe he was straying a little close to temptation, but he thought of Ruth and Boaz, and although he didn't necessarily understand or know all of the Old Testament rituals that might have allowed that, there was still the fact that Ruth had lain at Boaz's feet all night and it hadn't been considered wrong.

He didn't think the Lord would want him to not comfort someone who needed it, and while he didn't want to believe that he was not susceptible to temptation, he was pretty sure that wouldn't be an issue. Not with Gladys as vulnerable and grief stricken and overwhelmed as what she was.

It probably wasn't the best decision he'd ever made in his life, but he wasn't going to turn down someone who was grieving and needed comfort. Especially not a friend.

He opened his back door and held it for her to walk through first.

He flipped on the small light and pointed to a door off the kitchen.

"There's a bathroom right there, if you need it. I'm going to go grab a couple blankets and pillows." He nodded toward the open doorway. "The living room's right there."

By the time he came back downstairs, Gladys had her shoes off and was standing in the middle of the living room holding the puppy. She hadn't turned any lights on, but with the glow from the kitchen, he could see tear tracks running down her cheeks.

They hurt his heart and made his fingers clench in the blankets.

She was tough and strong and fierce and everything he admired, but this vulnerability was precious to him as well. From what she said, he guessed not many people got to see it.

Maybe that just made him the right person in the right place at the right time, or maybe that made him a real friend.

He wasn't sure, and he supposed he didn't want to dissect it too much. He didn't want to be disappointed.

Because he had the feeling that Gladys meant a lot more to him than what she should.

He spread the blanket out on the couch but kept the pillow in his hand.

"I figured you'd lie down, and I'd hold your head in my lap. I'll keep an eye on the puppy too, in case she needs to go out. I hope you're not a light sleeper."

"I can't imagine I'll sleep tonight, and...you're sleeping sitting up?"

He nodded.

"Okay." It wasn't like her to meekly give in without arguing, and he almost smiled. But then she turned her head, and her tear tracks glistened again.

Without saying anything, he walked to the bathroom, getting the small garbage can and the box of tissues that sat on the back of the toilet, bringing them into the living room and setting them on the small coffee table he pulled close enough to be within arm's reach of the couch. She sat down with the blanket and pup.

He settled down at the end where her head would be, and she lay down with her back to the outer edge of the couch, her head pressing against his stomach and her arm going around his back.

He didn't have his guitar, hadn't even thought about bringing it out from where he kept it in what was supposed to be the dining room but he'd kind of turned into his office/workspace, putting a desk in there and keeping his guitar and few music books, a bookshelf, and his gun cabinet.

Sometimes on the long North Dakota winter evenings when he wasn't working in the garage, he spent some time improving his skills or just playing for fun.

Growing up, he'd sung in church and school at times, but since he'd become an adult, he'd never sung in front of people. Still, this seemed like the kind of situation that called for a little musical comfort. So he started to sing softly while keeping one hand with his fingers in her hair and the other lightly rubbing her arm.

The puppy had snuggled down between Gladys's stomach and the couch and with a groan had gone straight back to sleep.

Silas figured it was his job tonight to look after these two girls, so different, but each maybe feeling a little lost and alone and scared. Maybe they just needed his calmness and maybe he could lend them a little of his strength, as long as he held tightly to the Lord.

There's a land that is fairer than day,And by faith we can see it afar;For the Father waits over the wayTo prepare us a dwelling place there.

In the sweet by and by,We shall meet on that beautiful shore;In the sweet by and by,We shall meet on that beautiful shore.

We shall sing on that beautiful shoreThe melodious songs of the blessed;And our spirits shall sorrow no more,Not a sigh for the blessing of rest.

To our bountiful Father above,We will offer our tribute of praiseFor the glorious gift of His loveAnd the blessings that hallow our days.

In the sweet by and by,We shall meet on that beautiful shore;In the sweet by and by,We shall meet on that beautiful shore.

By the time he was finished, the puppy snored softly, and Gladys had seemed to relax. He suspected she wasn't asleep. He doubted she had been able to calm down and fall asleep that quickly.

"That was beautiful," she whispered softly, her face pressed so closely against him he could feel her lips move against his stomach.

"I happen to know all the words to that one. But they seemed fitting too."

"Yeah. A lot of the songs I know are love songs, and they don't really apply to this right now. Maybe some are about being strong, but I don't even really want to be strong on my own. Is that terrible?"

"Not at all. I think there's a lot of emphasis on that in today's world. You know, being strong and standing on your own two feet and all that, but God wants us to need Him. All the time. Not just when bad things are happening, like you pointed out earlier. And it's not a weakness to do that. It's actually a strength, because it's hard."

"Yeah. It's easier to have physical comfort than it is to go to a God that I know isn't very happy with the way I've lived my life so far."

"He wants you." Silas didn't say anything more than that. It was simple but enough.

"I can't imagine why."

"I can."

She shivered.

"Are you cold?" he asked immediately.

"No." She didn't elaborate.

She lay there for a bit, and he could almost feel her tensing again. "Talk to me please."

"The silence is too hard?"

"Yeah. Sing. Talk. Something."

"I guess you know it's just my dad raising my brothers and my little sister and me. I wasn't very old when my mom walked out. I know it's not the same as what you're going through now, because I wondered why she didn't love me enough to take me with her or to stay. I guess when you're little, things like that look real simple. Like, she just needed to be nice to Dad, they needed to get along, and she just needed to keep doing what she'd been doing."

He shrugged a little, since he wasn't even really sure what he was saying. "I don't know. Just... I know it's hard to lose a parent."

"I wasn't even that close to my parents. I mean, I know I'd been living with them. Although I still have my own apartment in LA. Actually I share it with two other people. One of them's coming up." She paused. "She said she was, anyway."

"Then she'll be here," he said.

"No. Sometimes she just says things she knows people want to hear. She'll probably text me tomorrow and say she couldn't make it. She'll text me, because she won't want to tell me on the phone tonight. I can't judge that too harshly though, since I've done the exact same thing."

Her head moved just slightly as though she were restless. "Seems like a simple thing. Lying to make someone feel better, or lying because it's easier than saying, holy smokes, there's no way I'm flying to the middle of nowhere just for you when I haven't seen you in six months and don't really care to now, either."

"That would be me," he said, a little humor in his voice. He allowed it, because grief was easier to bear if there was laughter in there too.

She huffed, maybe a little laugh. "Yeah. That would be the truth, but some people, they're just not being honest, you know?"

"Yeah. There's a way to be honest and kind too. Usually. Although, it's always right to be honest."

"Yeah. So, while I hope she comes, I guess I'm not counting on her being here."

"You said you had more friends?"

"Yeah. But... None that I can depend on like you."

That last line had been uttered softly, almost as though she were a little embarrassed to admit it. He supposed Gladys wasn't any better at showing her emotions than he was.

"One good thing is my parents aren't going to be pushing me to get married anymore. In fact, they were bringing two men back with them for me to meet tomorrow. I told you about it. I guess I don't have to worry about that anymore." Now her voice held humor but also sounded very, very sad.

"Guess not," he said. He didn't find it quite as funny as she did. She still had to find someone.

"If I'm inheriting my parents' fortune, even if I have to share it with Mabel, I don't need to worry about the fortune my grandmother left."

"True."

She yawned, and he thought that was a good sign. A sign that maybe the problems that she had in front of her weren't looking quite as big as they had been. Or sharing them with him made it easier. Whatever it was, he was just happy to help.

Chapter Six

Finally realizing that what your partner does or says has nothing to do with you. It is them. It is their obscured vision. Pay no attention and happy co-existence is entirely possible.
- Patrice Gitaitis

Gladys came awake slowly.

Where was she?

It took a few more seconds, then the events of the previous night came rushing back.

The phone call. The news. The feeling of reeling and falling and not having any solid anchor. The need to hold on to someone or something.

Phone calls to friends, who were very sympathetic but not eager to make the trip to North Dakota.

Knowing there was one person she could depend on. Knowing he would probably still be up. Knowing it was just a matter of driving to him.

So she did.

Her parents. Gone.

Today... Today she would have to identify them. Tell her sister. Make funeral plans. Figure out where she was going to bury them. The list felt endless, and she wanted to groan.

Sadness overwhelmed her, and she closed her eyes again, pushing back the pain and the grief and all the feelings she didn't want to feel.

And then, she remembered where she was sleeping and who she was sleeping on. And wanted to groan even more.

She moved her head just a little, fairly certain that was a wet spot of drool on the bottom of his T-shirt.

Not that he would care. Not that he would say anything, but it was still embarrassing. She didn't like to be caught not at her best.

But coming to Silas had been a good idea. She couldn't remember waking up at all after falling asleep to his singing.

She moved her head a little more, and a big hand came down on top of it, stroking her hair and somehow pushing the frantic thoughts about her day aside.

Something squirmed against her chest, and she realized the puppy had worked its way down between herself and the couch. It snored softly.

"Good morning," Silas murmured.

"My eyes aren't open. How do you know I'm awake?"

"You usually talk in your sleep?"

"I didn't talk before you said good morning."

"Your breathing changed."

He noticed that? Maybe he'd done nothing else but sit awake all night, listening to her breathe.

"Did you sleep at all?" she asked, tilting her head a little so she could look up at him. His head was angled down, his eyes on the hand that stroked her hair back from her forehead.

Her hair.

She wondered if he would close his eyes while she got up. She'd be a mess. Her hair a mess, her breath stinky, and drool stuck to her mouth.

"Some."

She wondered if that meant five minutes or five hours.

"I know you did. I took the pup out twice. You didn't move either time."

"You could have left me here and gone upstairs and been comfortable in your bed."

"I guess I could have. But I didn't want you to wake up in an unfamiliar place and not know where I was."

"I'm an adult... But I appreciate it." She had been going to protest that she wasn't a child who was going to wake up and be scared, but the whole reason she was here at his house was because she couldn't handle her life by herself.

"Thanks for your consideration," she added softly.

His hand paused mid-stroke, then went back to smoothing her hair. "I don't want to rush you, but when you're ready to get up, I'll grab the pup and take her outside."

"Okay. I'm ready, I guess. Although, I'm not sure what I'm going to need to do today. I've...never done this before."

"Me either. But as long as you want me, I'll do it with you, and we'll figure it out."

His words eased the tight pull in her chest, giving her a bit of relief. She wasn't going to have to do this alone.

"I need to tell Mabel as soon as she gets up. She's usually up early."

Her sister Mabel was an introvert who had shunned the LA lifestyle. In fact, she'd shunned pretty much everything her parents were and was taking classes online, content to be at home.

She'd always been shy and quiet, pretty much the opposite of Gladys, and Gladys definitely felt protective toward her. Even if she couldn't relate to her personality.

"Sounds good. If we get some time, I'd like to swing around the church in Sweet Water and talk to the ladies about the pup and see if someone has lost one."

"Of course. Let's make sure we make time to do that." She moved, starting to sit up. The idea that she was going to be dealing with her parents' deaths still hadn't really sunk in. It felt surreal.

"You okay?" Silas asked as he caught the pup and snuggled it in his arms.

"Yeah." She put her hand to her hair. She supposed it didn't matter what she looked like because it was just Silas. "I feel like I'm walking around in an alternate reality. I know I'm supposed to be grieving, but I just feel numb."

"Maybe the numbness is your body's way of protecting you. You have a lot of things on your plate you have to do. Losing both parents at once is hard. Don't fight the numbness. Let your body do for you what it needs to."

That made sense. It just bothered her that she wasn't having a normal grief reaction. But then, what he'd said yesterday about everyone having a different normal rang in her head. "Maybe once I see the bodies. I'll probably fall apart then."

"That's fine. I'll be there."

She forgot about her hair and the drool that was probably stuck all over her face and looked at him, giving him a little smile. "Thank you. Thank you for last night... I wouldn't have slept like that if I'd been home. I can't believe how deeply I slept."

"I can't either." There was a little flash of teeth, then he looked down at the pup. "Especially considering I got up twice. I think you needed that."

She thought he was right. Again, maybe it was just her body taking care of her, knowing today was going to be a big day and she needed the rest. Or maybe that was just fanciful thinking on her part. It was hard to tell.

"I'm gonna want to take a shower, but I think I'll need to wait until we get to my house. I didn't think to bring any clothes."

"You can borrow some of mine if you don't want to wait. Whatever."

She didn't feel particularly dirty, but the idea of a shower waking her up, giving her some time to think and just feeling good with the water hitting her body, and...maybe it was a little bit of procrastination.

"If you don't mind, I'd love that."

"Mind holding her while I run upstairs?" He held the pup out.

Gladys took her without saying anything. Like she would mind holding a puppy.

He jogged out of the room and took the stairs two at a time.

Gladys watched him go, admiring the smooth grace with which he always moved. It reminded her of her car and how it handled sweet and smooth.

Thinking of her car, she had the sudden urge to throw up. She'd probably get more details about her parents' accident today, but what she had been doing on Friday nights hadn't been safe, and it could have been her who had run into a couple, killing them.

Right then, she vowed she'd never race her car again.

Hard on the heels of that thought was the one that racing had been what had kept her around Silas. If she didn't race anymore, she might not see him again.

And the idea of pulling away from him was almost more than she could handle. He'd been a rock since she'd stepped into his garage last night.

Lord, he said it was okay for me to depend on You, even though I haven't paid much attention to You.

She didn't know what else to say, and Silas came down the stairs just as fast as he went up.

"These will be big, but they're clean at least," Silas said as he handed his clothes to her, and she handed the puppy back over after kissing her on the head.

His fingers touched her arm and left a trail of sparks that shot up and down her backbone. Odd, because along with those sparks came a comforting warmth.

Attraction and comfort. She wasn't used to the combination and wasn't sure what to do about it. If anything.

"Thanks," she murmured, turning without looking at him again and heading to the bathroom she'd used the night before.

She shook her head a little. She must be more upset than what she thought, since she'd been thinking about him and totally forgotten her bedhead and all the other things that made it obvious that she'd just woken up. Not to mention, she had missed the wet spot on his T-shirt where she drooled on him.

Not appealing.

Still, after a shower she felt better, even if she didn't have any clean underthings. At least his clothes were clean and smelled good.

"Is it going to be a problem if I take the puppy with us?" Silas asked as she walked into the kitchen which smelled like bacon.

"I don't think so. I... I guess I'll probably have to go to the funeral home, but it shouldn't be a problem if we're holding her?"

Silas shrugged. "I doubt Henry will mind, but if he does, we can just talk outside." He indicated the skillet. "I thought you might not be hungry, but I cooked stuff for you anyway."

She hadn't expected that, and it made her smile. Kayla usually had things set out for breakfast, but just pastries and fruit.

"Are there eggs to go with the bacon?" she asked. To her surprise, her stomach rumbled.

"Sure. They're hot too."

"Coffee?" She wasn't quite as addicted to it as her roommates were, but it would probably give her a little boost she could really use today.

"I don't even have any in the house. Sorry. We can run by the C-Store before we head out to your place."

She nodded. "If you don't mind. I think I could use it today." She tilted her head. "You don't like coffee?"

"I guess I just don't like being addicted to stuff. Needing it. I'd rather have everything I need right here." He made a gesture that indicated himself.

"That's funny. Last night, you were telling me that we were supposed to depend on God."

"He's here too. The Bible says when you're saved, the Holy Spirit dwells within you. It also talks about our bodies being the temple of the Lord. I guess that's another reason not to be addicted to something. I'm not taking very good care of my temple if I have to feed it with an addiction every day."

"So you're telling me coffee isn't spiritual?" She smiled despite the gravity of the day. Seriously, sometimes religious people were just nuts.

"I could probably make an argument for that, couldn't I?" The grin on his face told her he was kidding.

"You could probably make an argument for anything, if you twist words well enough."

"Some people are experts at that."

She shrugged a shoulder, not wanting to go down that road. She could twist things pretty well, too. She had, as a teen. Twisted her parents' words, making them feel guilty and getting them to let her do what she wanted.

That had come back to bite her because she was the one who felt guilty now.

For the first time, her throat closed, and she felt like she might cry. She fought the feeling, because she didn't want to spend the entire day with tears streaming down her face.

"It's hitting you?" Silas asked, turning with a plate of eggs and bacon in one hand and grabbing two pieces of toast from the plate on the counter with the other.

"I guess. Just a memory. I wasn't always very kind to my parents. I'd guilt-trip them. Now I'm the one who feels guilty."

He nodded, but unlike a woman who might give her sympathy, he said, "I've done some things like that. I guess now in the back of my head, I'm always thinking, I don't want to live with regrets, so how am I going to do this so that twenty years from now, I'm not wishing I would have done things differently." He chuckled, no humor attached. "I'm not always successful in changing my behavior, but it makes me think anyway."

"I'm so much better at shoving the gas to the floor, just ripping ahead without thinking. I don't usually stop to think to change my behavior." She took the plate and set it down at one of the places that had been set with silverware. "It would probably be something good for me to learn to do."

"Self-control. Definitely a good idea."

Anytime they'd talked before, it had always been at the garage, usually about cars, although they'd had some deep discussions at times, which is part of what made Gladys always want to come back.

He had thoughts and ideas that made her think.

They finished eating with the conversation flowing easily between them with stretches of silence that didn't feel awkward. Just enough talking to keep Gladys's mind from whirling and running away from her.

After stopping at the C-Store and getting a coffee, they drove to her house.

The closer they got, the more her stomach felt like a mangled ball of wire, melting down.

Chapter Seven

Communication and the determination to stay together whatever life throws at you whether individually or as a couple.
- Laura Rose from Springfield, Illinois

As Silas drove up the long, paved drive toward the huge two-story columned house, Gladys could see that Mabel was already up and sitting on the front porch, her books spread out around her, a tablet in her hand.

Spring semester was over, but she was taking summer courses. Her hope was to be an equine vet. Which had upset her parents in equal measure: her dad because he wanted his girls to work in the business, and their mom because she didn't feel that was a fitting job for a lady.

Mabel hadn't cared and had done what she usually did, which was not say anything, just put her head down, and do whatever it was she decided to do.

Gladys had always been a little jealous of Mabel's ability to just move on, unruffled by whatever drama was going on around her, putting her nose in a book and blocking out the world.

She didn't seem to stress or strive about anything and didn't seem to have Gladys's restlessness, her need for speed, danger, and excitement.

Mabel's head lifted from her books, and she took her glasses off as Silas pulled to a stop and parked.

"I'll come with you, stand beside you, unless you tell me that you'd rather do something on your own. My goal is to make things easier for you, so you're not going to hurt my feelings if you'd rather I stay out of the way."

Gladys glanced across the console at Silas who studied her seriously. "I appreciate the consideration. I would definitely like you to be with me now." She looked at the puppy in her lap. "And this little girl too. She might help."

She had no idea how her sister was going to take this. Probably she'd be quiet and maybe even unemotional. After all, she couldn't remember the last time Mabel had an emotional outburst.

"I know that we might not keep the puppy, but we should think of a name for her. It's weird to just keep calling her the puppy. If we wind up keeping her, that'll be her name."

The words were out of her mouth, and she had reached for the door handle when she realized what she was saying. *We.*

Like the puppy was hers and his, too.

He had said she could have it, but he hadn't said anything about joint custody.

Shaking her head at herself, annoyed at her brain for coming up with the weirdest things, she supposed she should be grateful too. At least it was keeping her mind occupied on other things so she wasn't thinking about death. And the fact that she was an orphan.

She stumbled as she got out, the thought rocking her. She might be twenty-four, but she hadn't thought she'd be launched into life with no parents. That they were gone. Truly.

She wouldn't have said she liked them all that much, wouldn't have said they were close, wouldn't have even said they were much of a family, but she hadn't realized how much her parents had buffered her.

Silas met her more than halfway around the pickup. "Are you going to be okay?"

"I have a feeling you're going to be saying that a lot today," she said, sounding a little breathless. "I just realized I'm an orphan." She kept her voice low so it wouldn't carry to Mabel, who had set her book aside and stood up. Her brows scrunched down, as though she knew it was weird that Gladys was getting out of someone else's vehicle this early in the morning.

"Hey, Mabel," Gladys said as she walked up the stairs, grateful for the silent man beside her.

"I didn't notice you left here this morning," Mabel murmured, her eyes going to Silas, then the puppy, then back to Gladys.

"This is Silas Powers. He fixed a flat for me a few years ago, and we've been...friends since." That was true. Even if she did stumble over the word "friends."

Why was that so hard?

"I'm Mabel," Mabel said, holding out her hand. Her voice steady and level, like it always was.

Gladys had the thought that maybe she should have warned Silas that Mabel wasn't emotional. And maybe both of them would not have typical reactions to their parents' accident.

"I... I wasn't home last night."

"I didn't figure you'd gotten up before me. But I hadn't noticed you weren't here."

Usually they parked in the back, and Mabel probably didn't look outside for a car, since Mabel was usually up before Gladys anyway.

Maybe she should have spent more time trying to think of what she was going to say. Because she really had no idea. She just opened her mouth and started talking.

"I got a phone call last night after you went to bed. It was the North Dakota State police."

Mabel's forehead wrinkled. Her breath seemed to catch, and her mouth opened just a little. But other than that, there was no reaction. She didn't even urge Gladys on, just allowed her to continue at her own pace.

"Mom and Dad were on their way to the airport when another vehicle crossed the line and hit them head-on. Both of them were killed instantly."

Mabel blinked, then blinked again. Her mouth closed. And, not surprising to Gladys, she skipped right over the big dramatic reaction, and her first words were, "So where are the bodies? Are we planning their funeral today? Do you know who we need to call to get in touch with them?" Then she paused for a moment. "Were they sure they were our parents?"

That last question made Gladys's head tilt. "I don't know. I didn't think to ask that. I guess... I have a number I need to call that will put me in touch with... I can't remember, but they'll give us information on where the bodies are, and I guess we'll identify them, although I have to admit I'm not real clear. I suppose we'll just figure it out as we go."

Mabel nodded, still not looking particularly upset. That was Mabel. Maybe she had meltdowns in private, or maybe she just had a lot going on in her head that no one could see, but Gladys was far less surprised at her lack of reaction than she was at her own.

"There are a lot of things to think about," Mabel finally muttered.

"There are. But Silas told me last night when I was talking to him that we don't have to do it all at once. We have time. Just one thing at a time."

Mabel's eyes went to Silas as she nodded, her face completely preoccupied. "That's a good idea. It's overwhelming to think of all the things at once. Bodies first."

"You can...grieve first if you need to." Silas spoke before Gladys could answer.

She touched his arm, ready to tell him that this was Mabel. She was like deep water. Whatever was going on underneath, he couldn't tell on the surface.

But she hadn't gotten her mouth open before Mabel spoke. "I'm not going to fall apart, and I don't want to grieve right now. So I'm not going to."

Silas's brows went up, like he'd never seen anyone that calm before. Which Gladys found rather amusing, in a morbid sort of way she supposed, since Silas himself was not an emotional person.

He nodded at her declaration, respecting her right to grieve how she wanted, just like he told Gladys last night.

Mabel was all business, looking expectantly at Gladys, then her eyes shot back to Silas.

"Does the puppy have something to do with this?" she asked, as though somehow her parents had left them a puppy when they passed.

"No. I found her along the side of the road yesterday. I need to ask around and see if she belongs to anyone, but for now, she's available if you need her." Silas didn't say if she needed to cuddle, but she supposed Mabel might be more interested in hugging the dog than she was in hugging people, and sure enough, Mabel simply held her hands out for the animal, and Silas silently handed her over.

The pup squirmed a little, probably wanting down to play, but Mabel had a way with animals, and she calmed down in her arms.

She settled in, snuggling up, while Mabel cradled her, putting her head down to kiss the top of the pup's head.

The next few hours were a blur. Not because they were so busy, but just because things were finally sinking in.

Gladys fielded a few phone calls from her dad's business, but just a few, since once news got out, people were respectful of their grief.

They called to take care of the bodies, and Henry, the funeral home director, said he would meet them at the funeral home after he got his hay in.

That made Gladys smile, since it was only in North Dakota that they couldn't plan a funeral until the funeral director made his hay.

"It won't make any difference whether we do it now or whether we do it this evening, but it'll make a big difference for my hay, since we're supposed to have thunderstorms tonight and a possible tornado," Henry had said.

After she had gotten off the phone, Silas had murmured that he inherited the funeral home from his mother's side of the family and his consideration for the grief-stricken could use a little improvement. But Henry was also used to dealing with the hearty folks of North Dakota, who accepted the death of someone as a matter of course.

They didn't tiptoe around it the way some areas of the country might.

Gladys had already known that. At least in theory.

Maybe, with her counseling degree, she should offer some type of support to Mabel, but Mabel was one of the strongest people she knew, and if anything, Mabel would be supporting her.

The bodies had been delivered to the funeral home, and they sat around the house, fielding a few visits as word got around and folks showed up with casseroles and condolences.

Silas drove Mabel and Gladys to the funeral home, getting there a few minutes early, but Henry was waiting. Silas stood beside them while they identified the bodies of their parents.

That was definitely the hardest thing. Although, talking about the funeral, and what they were going to do with the bodies, and all of the details that surrounded death were the things that finally made it real.

No matter what her relationship with her parents, they were still her parents and they would never be back. She would never be able to roll her eyes at her mother's snobbery or wish for her dad to take some time off work and spend it with her.

Never have that comfort of knowing there was a place to go for the holidays, where she'd spent every one of her childhood. She'd never have the luxury of choosing whether she wanted to go to a friend's place and spend them there or go home.

She supposed she'd been like most people and figured her parents would always be there, so she chose her friends more often than not.

Now she didn't have a choice.

It was eight o'clock that evening when they walked out of the mortuary after planning the combined funeral and taking care of so many little details she felt drained and exhausted, and that's when everything hit her.

She was crying before they'd made it to the car.

Silas, who'd kept an arm around her most of the day, noticed immediately.

He didn't say anything, just stopped and pulled her closer.

He'd been holding the pup while Mabel and she had talked to Henry, so

Mabel had both hands free, and when she noticed Gladys crying, she wrapped her sister in a hug.

Which made Gladys cry harder.

It wasn't the kind of thing that felt like she'd be able to cry about once and have it be over. She felt like she was walking through a dark cloud and would never come out on the other side.

Almost hopeless.

Chapter Eight

Similar beliefs, trust in God and working to see things from the other person's point of view.
- Jean Hall from Ohio

Mabel dropped her arms and stood back, always uncomfortable with displays of emotions.

Silas felt like he'd figured her out a little over the course of the day.

He handed the puppy to her. She took it, almost eagerly, which made Gladys smile through her tears.

But then Mabel snuggled down with the puppy, burying her nose in her fur and closing her eyes, and somehow the sight made Gladys cry again, harder. Sobs this time.

Silas wrapped both of his arms around her and pulled her head into his shirt.

"I already soaked one shirt of yours today," she said between sobs and hiccups.

"It's okay," Silas murmured, one hand stroking down her back, the other one holding her firmly against him. "That's what I'm wearing it for."

"For me to cry into?"

"That's right," he said, and there might have been a touch of humor in his voice, since he'd also figured out over the course of the day and last night, if he hadn't known it before, that even though she was sad, she still wanted to be able to laugh. To joke. To not be consumed with grief the way she was now.

"I can't believe they're really gone. I think I heard it last night and just... didn't believe it."

"Sometimes we need to start believing this kind of thing in stages. We just can't accept the whole big mess at one time."

Chapter Nine

Forgiveness, trust, willing to help and work with each other. Having a belief system you both trust in makes a big impact too!
- Vandy Dodge from Lake Stevens, WA

Silas held her while she cried, and Gladys appreciated it. Maybe she was taking advantage of his kindness, but she didn't hurry and allowed herself to cry as much as she needed to. After all, Silas had said that morning that her body was taking care of her. Maybe it knew she needed to cry now.

It was a long time before she pulled away, swiping at her cheeks with her hands and seeing the big wet spot she'd left on Silas's shirt.

"I'm sorry," she said, her voice husky from her tears.

His hand reached out, swiping carefully at her cheek, wiping away some wetness she'd missed, with the pad of his thumb. Gently. So gently it almost made her start crying again. And she would have sworn she had no tears left.

"I think you needed that," he said, his voice as gentle as his hand had been.

She nodded, not knowing what to do with the swirling feelings in her chest. Hurt, but also peace and tenderness and that same attraction, all mixed with her grief.

Clearing her throat, she looked over at where Mabel sat on the ground, the puppy jumping and playing around her while she used a piece of grass to tickle the animal's nose and give her something to bite.

It looked like a scene from a park, not a funeral home, but Gladys knew her sister well enough to see that her heart really wasn't in playing with the puppy, which was unusual, since her parents had never allowed them to have animals, and any time Mabel could be around any creature, her eyes lit up and her whole body seemed animated.

"I think I'm better. I think I can make it home, or you can take me to your house so I can pick up my car." She looked up at him, hating to ask but knowing she was going to anyway. "Would you stay at our house tonight?"

He looked down at her, his eyes deep and unfathomable. She couldn't imagine anyone else with the patience to do what he had done today, which was step back when he wasn't needed and move forward when he was, sharing his puppy, his car, his shirt, and anything else that she needed from him.

"I need to stop at my house and get some clothes. So I don't have to borrow yours in the morning." His eyes twinkled just a bit, although his face remained serious.

"Thank you."

They gathered Mabel up and stopped at Silas's house to grab not just clothes but some things for the puppy, including food.

"Tomorrow, I'm definitely going to need to get her some food and also talk to the Piece Makers, which I didn't get a chance to do today."

He'd had plenty of time when they sat inside the house, waiting on phone calls or just staring off into space, but he hadn't left her. She appreciated that.

"I think I can handle tomorrow by myself."

She didn't think any such thing, but she couldn't ask him to take off work indefinitely and be her buffer. "I thought I was going to have a couple of friends coming, but they all canceled on me."

"North Dakota is a long way from California." He shrugged, like it wasn't a big deal her friends didn't care enough to come. "I'll be here. I already told my brothers I wouldn't be working."

"You didn't have to do that. Really. I...I can do it on my own." But she knew the words didn't sound confident. She might as well have said, *please stay with me.*

"You can tell me to leave if you want to, but how about I stay the night, then we'll go from there. How's that?"

She nodded, and maybe the expression on her face showed him how grateful she was. "I feel like I've aged a million years in the last three days."

"I think sometimes we go through things, and they either make us better, and we learn things, or we spiral off, looking for something to numb the pain, or make things easier, instead of facing the hard stuff."

She knew exactly what he was talking about. Pills would have made today a lot easier. Alcohol too. She could party tonight and completely forget that she had any responsibilities at all.

Those ideas might have been tempting.

"Is it not facing reality if I want to watch a little mindless TV?" She smiled some, pretty sure that she wasn't going to be able to be swept away by mindless TV. What she really wanted was for Silas to sing to her again.

"Should I bring my guitar?" he asked, and she couldn't believe how easily he read her mind.

"Do you mind?"

"If you can stand to listen to me sing, I don't mind at all."

"I'd like that. Thank you."

Chapter Ten

Paying attention to your husband and the little things going on with him, even when many other people and responsibilities are clamoring for your attention, will go a long way toward making a marriage last.
- Beverly from Georgia

"I think that's enough for tonight."

Silas lifted his guitar off his lap and reached over, leaning it against the side table where he'd been keeping it at night for the last week since he'd been staying at the LeFrak girls' house.

"Thanks for singing." Mabel stretched and stood from the chair that she'd been snuggled in with Pansy, which is what they'd named the puppy. "I'm going to head up after I take Pansy out."

She strode toward the kitchen and the back porch, where Pansy had her own special spot just off the walk.

"Good night, sis," Gladys said softly.

"Good night."

Mabel walked out, leaving them in comfortable silence.

"Thanks for being there today. It wasn't as hard as I thought it was going to be." Gladys moved, adjusting her position on the couch so she could lie down with her head in his lap, which had become their regular position since her parents had died.

He wasn't sure why she was thanking him. He'd stayed beside her as much as she'd needed him to for the last week.

Actually, she'd spent several days beside him, since she'd come to the garage with him while he had worked on the trucks that had come in.

His brothers and his dad had been understanding, if maybe a little baffled, since they hadn't even known that Gladys and he were friends. But they hadn't questioned anything. He was an adult for one. But also, he'd always put in more than his share of the work. Always had done more than was required, always stayed late if something needed to be finished, and never quit a job until it was done right.

They wouldn't begrudge him a few days to help a friend through a hard time.

But he did need to get back. Spending all this time with Gladys had not been good for him. It had just made him want more. After standing with her at the funeral today, it had been even more obvious that they didn't belong together.

He recognized some of the people there. State and national politicians. Business people and influencers famous on social media. Hollywood celebrities.

Funny how the important people came for the funeral, but tonight it was just the two women and him.

Surface friendships, nothing deep.

The town of Sweet Water would have rallied around them more, but he figured most people had been intimidated by all the big names and had given perfunctory condolences, not really knowing either Mr. or Mrs. LeFrak, and moved on, assuming the girls had plenty of friends surrounding them to keep them company.

That's the way he would have been.

Only one of Gladys's girlfriends had made it in, and she didn't even stay one night.

"You handled things pretty well today," he said softly, since they hadn't really talked about it. Mabel had been there, and they'd talked in general terms about the funeral and the people who came to pay their respects. They hadn't had a graveside service, but Silas and Mabel and Gladys had driven together to the grave to watch the coffins lowered.

"I've leaned on you more than I should have. You're the perfect support. You step up when I need you and move back when I don't."

He'd tried. He'd tried to be exactly what she needed, no more. Not that he would spend his life doing that for someone, but at a time like this, when he was just trying to help, to him that was the best way.

"You haven't really leaned on me at all." He felt like she had been strong on her own. And he had just lent a little support. Not like a crutch or anything.

"You have no idea." She snuggled down, putting her head on his leg the way she had done each night before. The same woman who raced fearlessly for the last year or so on Friday nights was the one who lay on his leg now. He couldn't say he didn't like it. Actually, he liked it too much.

Way too much.

He hadn't wanted to leave before the funeral, but now...

"I know what I see, and I see someone who's been poised and gracious. And strong." His hand stroked her hair. He admired her, loved watching her, and needed to go. "I didn't want to say anything before the funeral, because I knew today would be a hard day for you, but I think I probably ought not to stay here anymore."

She tensed. He could feel it through his leg. Her head jerked around so she was looking up at him. "Why not?"

He looked down, seeing her eyes full of questions, and knew she had absolutely zero idea of the fact that being around her so much, working with her so closely, dealing with all of the things that they had—her grief and planning and helping her sister, and his work and the puppy and everything that they'd done together—had made him...start to fall.

He was definitely developing feelings for Gladys, feelings beyond the attraction he'd already had. The more time he spent with her, the more time he wanted.

She didn't feel the same. She just looked at him as someone who could help her. Someone who was calm and steady and whom she could depend on.

She wasn't going to return his feelings, and he was going to end up hurt.

Not to mention, there was a fine line between giving her comfort and overstaying beyond what he should.

"You don't need me... I just think it's best," he finally said lamely. Not sure how to explain to her all the things that were in his head. All the reasons why seemed so reasonable and necessary to him, but he couldn't seem to get them to form intelligent sentences in order to convince her but not allow her to know he felt more than he should.

"I'm too needy," she said flatly, turning her head but not sitting up, although she didn't snuggle down under the blankets like she often did either. She just lay there, like she was staring at his stomach, frustrated with herself for not being stronger.

"No."

"No, I understand. Men hate clingy women. And I've been clingy. About as clingy as a person can get."

"You haven't. That's not it at all."

He racked his brain to try to figure out the words to tell her that he didn't want to fall for her. Maybe he should just come right out and say it.

He had never been very good at saying one thing and meaning another. He'd never been that kind of person. He opened his mouth to speak, but she said, "You're right. That's for the best. I'd tell you to go home tonight, but it's already late."

He'd made her angry. It wasn't in her tone necessarily, but her words were clipped. He wanted to reassure her. Let her know that it wasn't because of her, and it definitely wasn't because of her being clingy, it was because of him and how he was feeling, that he was feeling too much.

But he'd already given so much to her, allowed her to use his presence however she needed, watched her, and looked after her even while she slept.

He didn't want to expose himself still more.

"I don't know what to say. I like being here, making sure you're sleeping, chatting at night when you wake up. I feel like that's helped you, and I love that." He paused. "But I think you're ready to move on. You don't need me anymore."

That was true. She probably hadn't needed him as much as he'd been here. Tonight maybe, because of what she'd done today, but she'd been sleeping just fine. It had only been a night or two that she'd been restless. But that might have been more the puppy waking her up before Mabel started taking the pup with her.

"I suppose if you found a home for the puppy, you would have said something?" she finally asked, and her tone was a little more humble, less haughty.

"I'll talk to the Piece Makers tomorrow, but I haven't heard a thing."

It was possible that, because of the funeral, they hadn't wanted to say anything, since he'd seen several of them there, but he doubted it. If someone was looking for the dog, they wouldn't wait.

"I'm pretty sure we can bank on her being ours. Uh, yours."

She huffed out a breath that wasn't quite a laugh. "You don't have to give me your dog."

"I'm not giving it to you. Mabel seems to have commandeered her from both of us."

"Mabel always does that. We were never allowed to have animals, but anytime we went anywhere, Mabel became a surrogate mom to whatever animals they had until we left."

They talked a bit about Mabel and how she'd been snuggled up with the dog. It seemed to be the one thing that she could hold and touch easily. She was definitely an animal person more than a people person.

"I'm worried about her," Gladys said softly.

"She lives in her head a lot," Silas agreed. "Although I think sometimes it's hard for people who don't have a problem socializing to understand people who do."

He'd always had his brothers to run interference for him, since he wasn't a great socializer himself. As he'd gotten older, he'd gotten better. Sometimes he still didn't talk enough, but when he was paired up with someone like Gladys, who didn't have a problem talking, it worked out okay. And eventually he relaxed and could say what was on his mind.

Most of what was on his mind.

"I guess you're right. She seems fine on the outside, but I'm always concerned that people who seem fine to the rest of the world are actually struggling with something. I... I had a friend—a casual friend—who was very much like that. He ended up committing suicide. None of us had any idea he had any issues. He just never talked about them."

"I suppose that's a danger. I could see if my sister wants to talk to her. She's more her age." Although, he wasn't sure whether Sadie would have anything in common with Mabel or not. But he knew Sadie would talk to her because Sadie was always willing to help out.

"Your sister lost her mother very young. Maybe they'd have that in common," Gladys said thoughtfully.

He pulled the hair back away from her neck and felt her shiver. He'd figured out, over the hours that he'd spent running a hand over her back and hair and wherever just to try to ease her mind and offer comfort, that the back of her neck was very sensitive. Particularly just above the hairline.

Maybe it was cheating a little for him to have cataloged some of the things he knew she really liked, but he'd done it anyway, mostly because he enjoyed making her feel good but maybe a little selfishly because he wanted her to know that he *could* make her feel good.

"That's true. Although I suppose it's a little different when your mom walks out versus dying. Plus, Sadie was pretty young and never really knew Mom. But sometimes we can talk about our differences as easily as we can talk about our similarities."

He wished that were true for Gladys and him. But some differences were easier to get over than others. He and Gladys were so different, there was no middle ground.

"I'll take some time tomorrow to run into Sweet Water and talk to the Piece Makers about Pansy. I'll also say something to Sadie when she comes to work at nine."

"And I'll say something to Mabel. I hardly think she'll actually go in and talk to Sadie, but maybe she'd go in with me? I could stop in sometime?"

"That sounds good. You and I can hang out there for a little bit in case we need to break the ice with them. Although Sadie is pretty good at having one-sided conversations."

They lapsed into silence, and Gladys's breath became even.

Silas figured she was asleep and leaned back, staring at the ceiling, wishing he hadn't said that this would be his last night, when her voice spoke softly.

"I'm sorry I got a little snippy with you earlier. You're right. I know you weren't telling me that I was too clingy. I guess I just have that fear. I've always been taught I have to stand on my own two feet, that I can't depend on a man to help me, that women need to show that they're just as good if not better than men. It's almost like a burden that women carry. You know? We can't let our gender down by being needy or submissive or gentle. We have to be tough and strong and better than men."

"Wow. That's a big burden. I almost think men are taught the opposite. In some ways."

They chuckled softly at how upside down the world could get.

"I know you didn't mean it, anyway. I just... I'm just a little scared, and I didn't want to admit it."

"If you still need me, I'll be here. But...I know you can do it. I guess there's a temptation for me to want you to need me, and keep coming, and even to push to come. Because... It's a little bit of an ego boost, I guess. You needing me." It was more than that, but that was the truth. Just not all of it.

"If it's an ego boost, you deserve it. I never understood why you were always content to allow me to drive. After all, you were the one who did the work to the car."

"It was your car."

"I know. But didn't you ever want to drive?" She said it like that would be the only reason that he would go, to drive, and she just couldn't fathom anything else.

"No." It was the honest answer. "It was enough for me just to watch you. It's always fun to watch someone do something they love."

He thought that was a compliment, but she didn't say anything for a while, and he thought maybe he'd offended her. Maybe she thought he hadn't loved it as much as she did. Or maybe she was feeling self-conscious, knowing he had been watching her.

That was a little hard to believe. Gladys had never been the slightest bit shy or self-conscious, other than her outburst a little earlier about being afraid she was clingy.

"Can I say something?" she finally asked, just as he had been dozing off.

Chapter Eleven

Treat your husband better and more kindly than you treat your friends, co-workers, or clients.
- Beverly from Georgia

"Sure," Silas said, his voice a little rough, his eyes still closed as his head leaned on the back of the couch.

"After my parents were killed, I realized how many times I'd gone over the yellow line, how many times someone beside me has been in the completely wrong lane. I always feel like there's plenty of room, I can see far enough ahead, there's nothing to worry about, but...once it happens, you can't take it back."

"True," he said, a little bit of his sleepiness leaving him and some apprehension taking its place. If this was going where he thought it was going, he was definitely going to regret telling her he didn't want to stay with her anymore. Because he thought she was leading up to telling him that she didn't want to race anymore, which meant he wouldn't be seeing her.

The thought had his heart clenching in his chest.

"I guess I'm saying, I'm not going to be doing it anymore. I made that decision a week ago. I'm glad to hear that it wasn't something you love because I worried about telling you."

He waited to speak until he was sure his throat would work properly, since it tightened at her words.

"My love is working under the hood. There is something deeply satisfying about making a motor purr. Giving it power. Putting it on the ground. And watching someone who is good at handling it, which you are, is just a little bonus I don't usually get." He didn't add that being with her was something else he loved. "Truth be told, I'm happy you made that decision. It was dangerous, not to mention illegal. I fought with my conscience more than once over that part of it. In fact, every time we did it."

"You and your conscience?" She didn't say anything more, and he figured she was probably a little exasperated at him, since it wasn't just the racing that he fought over, but as far as he knew, she didn't know about anything else. But they were here on the couch, with him sitting up, because of his conscience.

"You don't have one?" he couldn't help asking. Was he the only person that was the slightest bit concerned about what God thought? About what He commanded?

"I do, but I've learned that I don't get struck by lightning when I cross it, so I assume that means God's okay with it."

He hesitated, then figured this was just like some of the other things they talked about. They didn't always agree. It was okay to not agree, and Gladys felt the same way.

"Just because judgment doesn't fall immediately doesn't mean God isn't displeased."

"You're saying judgment is coming?" she asked, not a flippant question but sounding thoughtful.

"It is. I don't have to say it. God already has."

The refrigerator condenser kicked on in the kitchen, the hum just background noise as he waited for her to speak.

Eventually, she said, "I want to say nothing like that has happened before. God's wrath. At least in our lifetime. Something that we can point to and say, yeah, God did this."

He wanted to point out there were tons of things that they could say were God's wrath. But he didn't. And she went on.

"But I was thinking about Noah building the ark. It says it took him a hundred years. In all that time, the earth had never seen rain. And yet there he was, building this big boat." She huffed out a breath. "It was sitting on dry ground. Way too big for anyone to move, even if there was a river or lake big enough nearby for it to float in."

Her fingers stretched out on his leg, and he held his breath. "I'm guessing there were a lot of people telling Noah he was a fool. That God's wrath wasn't coming. That there wouldn't be any judgment. That he was a crazy old man who believed in fairy tales and conspiracy theories."

Her fingers stopped moving, and Silas tried to breathe out without being obvious.

"And yet, Noah was right after all. And all those people who thought he was wrong felt the judgment of God."

"There are a lot of people who died." Silas had no idea how populated the earth was at that point, but with only eight people surviving, it was a lot of destruction.

"That's pretty serious about judgment. And I think we have a tendency to want to downplay that, because in our modern society, that seems almost barbaric."

"It does, but when you're the Creator of the universe, you get to make the rules."

"And yet, God is a loving God. So the rules have to be just."

"He's also merciful. He'll show mercy if you ask for it."

"That's what I'm counting on. I guess I said all of that to say, I made a little comment about your conscience, but I think you're right. I think you're right to be concerned about the things God's concerned about. And the commandments that He gives us. I think it's the rest of the world who is wrong. And... It was me too."

Her words made him glad that he hadn't been afraid to broach the subject. That he hadn't been afraid to talk about something that he thought they might not agree on.

"Good to know you think that. It's kind of uncommon."

"It might be a little bit of a stretch to apply the rule of sowing and reaping to mechanics, but I just think that you can't put water into the fuel tank and expect your car to run. You can't put cheap parts into it and not expect to get a cheap performance. Judgment is similar, since you can't expect to sin and not pay for it. Somehow."

He thought about the cross and how Christ had paid for the sins of the world. Just that sacrifice. But it had to be something that a person accepted. People who didn't would face the wrath of God.

"That's kind of a deep subject. For before bed anyway," he finally said.

"I guess death makes you think about things like that. I wasn't particularly close to my parents, you know that already, but that doesn't mean that losing them hasn't made me think and will probably change me in a lot of ways."

"That makes sense."

Her fingers started moving again, and as much as he liked it, he had a feeling it was a bad thing.

"I have to meet with the accountant tomorrow. He wanted to put the meeting off, but I want to figure things out. I... I know my parents have a place in LA, and... I'm not sure what to do."

"Which state to live in?"

"Yeah."

He'd known this might happen. Knew that when she said she wasn't racing again, he might not see her anymore, but he supposed he also knew that she might choose not to stay in North Dakota. Even people who were born in North Dakota sometimes chose not to stay. It wasn't an easy place to live.

"Silas?"

"Hmm?" he asked, his head back and his eyes closed again. He wasn't going to fight whatever God was ordering in her life. He'd known from the beginning that they most likely weren't going to end up together, and he needed to let go. Needed to be okay with it. Needed to let her do what she had to do while he continued to do what he knew God had placed in front of him.

"I never asked you the question I wanted to."

"You scared?" he asked, teasing.

If there was anything that Gladys wasn't, he could almost guarantee it would be scared.

His head raised slowly, and his eyes opened, although there wasn't much to see in the darkness of after midnight.

"Go on. I'll answer if I can."

"I guess I'm kind of counting on that." She took a breath. "I'm not racing anymore, and I need to make a decision about where I'm going to live, and it might not be here, but... I want to stay friends. You've literally been the best friend I've ever had. I don't want to lose that, and I also feel like I owe you."

"Friends don't keep score," he said. He didn't want her being kind to him or doing things with him, just because she felt like she owed him. The thought revolted him.

"No. Of course they don't. But you don't want to have a friendship that's lopsided either. Where one person is doing all the giving and one person is doing all the taking."

"That's just the way it's needed to be for the last week."

"Even before that. I know you said you loved working on my car, but I was really the one who was getting a lot out of our relationship, and you not so much."

"I disagree." But he didn't want to argue, so he answered her other question. "Of course. Of course I want to stay friends with you. After all, I don't have too many friends that I've sat with in the middle of the night, running my hand over their hair, talking about things that I don't talk about with anyone else. I want to keep you close."

He said the words lightly, because they were deep words and had the potential to be emotional words, and they were talking about friendship. Nothing more. He mostly wanted them to be friendship words.

She laughed. "You make this almost sound like fun. Sleeping practically sitting up, and watching me grieve. Having me drool on your shirt, seeing my bedhead in the morning."

"I didn't mind any of that. Now your morning breath on the other hand—"

"Oh, my goodness! I can't even believe you said that."

"Said? I feel like I need to post a warning for the rest of the world on a billboard or something."

"I can hardly refute it, because it's the truth. But I'm not worried, since you're not that kind of person."

"I was teasing you. I've never noticed any morning breath, I just heard you talk about it." And that was the truth. Even what she claimed was a bedhead looked cute to him.

"That's kind of you to say."

He could tell from her tone that she didn't believe him, but he didn't try to talk her into it. She knew that he didn't go around saying things that weren't true or giving compliments just to make someone feel good.

"So maybe you need to get a social media account so that we can stay friends." She shifted, rolling until she lay on her back, with her head looking up.

He glanced down but shook his head. "I'd rather see you in the flesh. I know that's not really the way the world works anymore, but anything less doesn't feel like friendship to me, if it's just on some piece of electronics. Not to mention, you can't do this." He patted her head. Reminding her that he'd been stroking her hair.

"True," she said, her voice thoughtful, subdued, and he imagined that maybe she was thinking about where she was deciding to live. "It's just that there aren't a lot of job opportunities in North Dakota."

"You think you're going to sell your parents' business?" he asked.

"I don't know. I guess I'll have to wait and see what the accountant says. I just know... I just know that I want to stay. But I have a feeling I'm not going to be able to."

There didn't seem to be anything for him to say about that, and he laid his head back down on the couch. He didn't want her to go, but he wasn't going to try to talk her into staying. It wasn't his place to try to get what he wanted or to try to make what he wanted be what was best for her.

He did say a small prayer though, that God would give her wisdom, and that if they were supposed to be together, which he highly doubted, that God would be clear.

Chapter Twelve

To make a marriage last, always focus on showing kindness and respect for the other person, even when you disagree. Don't take your spouse for granted.
- Sarah

"Mabel, this is Sadie," Silas said after they walked into the office that was attached to the side of the garage. "Sadie, this is Gladys's sister, Mabel."

The young ladies shook and smiled at each other, and as he suspected she would, Sadie started talking immediately. "Silas said that you're studying to be a veterinarian?"

Mabel nodded.

"That made me think of Lark Stryker. Dr. Stryker now, since she's finished her internship and come back to North Dakota to practice. She grew up here and has been back a couple of years. She actually has a bit of a girls' home going on. From what I understand, she hasn't gone out and searched for them, but people have asked her to take them, and she has. They help her take care of the animals and—"

"People just drop their kids off with her?" Mabel said incredulously. The fact that she spoke at all shocked Silas, and he met Gladys's eyes, sharing a look. She was just as surprised as he was.

"Kind of. I mean, it's not like they're not wanting their kid anymore. But you know how sometimes kids get into stuff they shouldn't? Or start running with the wrong friends? Lark had a friend from college who had a sister who had a daughter..." Sadie took a minute to laugh at that convoluted circle. "Anyway, she had a friend who knew someone whose daughter just needed a place to get away from the crowd she was running with." Sadie shrugged her shoulders. "Lark took her in, and word got around, I guess."

"Kids are expensive. I wonder where she's getting money? She wouldn't make that much being a vet in North Dakota?"

"I think someone in her family has money." Sadie furrowed her brows and looked at Silas.

He shrugged. "There was a rumor running around that they inherited something or married into money or something. I'm not sure exactly." He heard it was one of Lark's brothers that was financing her, but he couldn't remember where he'd gotten the money exactly.

"Anyway, since she's already a vet, and you're working toward it..."

"I wouldn't want to bother her. She sounds busy."

"She is. But I go out some. I enjoy cooking, and I know a little bit about gardening too, so I work with the girls a little, and she always appreciates it. I guess I wasn't suggesting that we go out to just visit. But if you have any spare time, I know that Lark would love to show you around and even just allow you to follow her so you can get some hands-on experience, if that's something that people who are working toward becoming a vet do?" Sadie raised her eyes, waiting, since she obviously had no idea.

Mabel looked extremely interested and moved closer, cuddling Pansy close to her.

Silas and Gladys raised their brows at each other again and smiled. She gave him a little thumbs-up sign.

Sadie and Mabel were so deeply in conversation, they didn't even bother to excuse themselves but slipped out of the room.

Silas closed the door quietly behind them as Gladys said, "That was a resounding success."

"I never even thought about Lark. That was brilliant. As much as I might not want to admit that my little sister is brilliant." Silas knew there was affection in his voice, and Gladys's face softened. He wasn't sure exactly what that look meant, but he figured she liked that he thought so much of his sister. He wasn't sure why though.

"I was gonna run over to the Piece Makers and ask about Pansy. You have time to come along?"

She glanced at her watch, and he remembered about the meeting she had with her accountant.

"I wish I could, but I have ten minutes until my meeting with the accountant. I know it's going to be more involved than what I want to get, but it has to be done."

"You need me?" he asked, but she shook her head.

"I appreciate it, but I know I'll be okay. I might not understand everything, but..." She laughed a little. "I know I'm not going to be blindsided like I was with the call from the police."

There was still a little sadness in her eyes, and there probably would be for a long time. No matter how close or how much she liked or didn't like her parents, there was just a part of a person that hurt when they died.

They separated at their cars, and Silas followed Gladys into town, waving as she pulled off the street in front of the diner. He kept going to the church and pulled into the back lot.

As much as he didn't want to think that someone would drop a puppy off along the road and abandon it, he was hoping that they hadn't found or heard of anyone who had lost one.

He held hope since Sadie had made posters for him, and he and Gladys had pinned them up in town, and they hadn't gotten a single call.

Mabel had really seemed to have gotten attached to the pup, although maybe if she found a new purpose with Lark and all the things she had going on, maybe it wouldn't be so hard on her if someone did claim Pansy.

Silas parked and got out of his truck, striding to the basement door, determined that whatever the outcome was, they would deal with it.

Chapter Thirteen

Putting your partner before your pride.
- Julie Young

"My sources say he's headed our way." Charlene looked up from her phone at her fellow Piece Makers.

"Your sources?" Vicki asked doubtfully.

Charlene gave her a look. "Jenny, at the salon."

"Oh," Vicki said, looking back down at the quilt she'd been folding, smoothing the rough edges and making sure every fold was perfect.

Charlene appreciated her attention to detail. It was part of what made her a good matchmaker. Of course, it helped in making quilts as well.

"Now, remember. Whatever you do, we cannot be obvious about the fact that we want him to get together with Gladys."

"I don't understand why not. If we want them to get together, let's just flat-out tell him they ought to be together." Teresa looked a little grumpy. She still hadn't quite recovered from her journey on the other side of the law from the last couple that they'd helped find each other. Plus, Teresa was very much a straight shooter.

She didn't understand the fine art of deceit.

"First of all, Gladys just lost her parents. That was an unexpected development, and it caused us to postpone the kissing we had planned in order to get them together. However, it's quite possible that Gladys will leave the state, and there goes the chance that Silas and she will ever be together. Now, as to why we can't flat-out tell them, it probably wouldn't be appropriate or socially acceptable for us to be pushing her into someone, even though we're under time constraints, but men especially do not like to be told what to do. You need to give them a thinly veiled suggestion. It doesn't have to be completely veiled, because normally they're not very good at insight, and then you have to give them a little nudge in the right direction."

Charlene smiled with satisfaction. It shouldn't be hard.

"In my experience, thinly veiled suggestions don't work. You need to flat-out say what you want, or a man just doesn't understand," Vicki said, giving the quilt another military-like precision fold.

"That's true for some men, but there *are* men with *some* discernment and a little bit of sensitivity. We're going to assume Silas is one of those." Charlene was fairly certain he was. The quiet ones usually were. It was the ones that wouldn't stop talking about themselves that a person pretty much had to hit over the head with a two-by-four to get them to listen.

The doorknob rattled.

"Ladies. Take your places," Charlene hissed under her breath, jerking her head away from the door and looking down at the sewing in her lap like she'd been doing it all morning.

As the door opened, she looked up, surprise on her features, which she allowed to give way to an expression of pleasure as she stood.

"Silas! What a surprise." Charlene smiled, ignoring Teresa's sour look. She wasn't lying. If she hadn't known he was coming, it would have been a surprise.

"Morning, ladies," Silas said, taking his hat off and holding it in one hand, casually, although his fingers fiddled with the brim, showing that he wasn't as completely at ease as he looked.

"Good morning, Silas," Kathy said, batting her lashes.

If Charlene were close enough, she would have elbowed her. She couldn't be flirting with the target even if he was devilishly handsome.

Silas nodded in reply, ignoring the flirting.

Charlene suppressed her nod of approval. She didn't care for a ladies' man, someone who flirted with everyone. Even if she didn't already know that about Silas, he'd checked off the right box in her head. She wouldn't match someone up if she thought he would ever have a wandering eye.

She didn't worry about Silas wandering anywhere. Gladys would be getting a good man, if they could pull this off.

"I was wondering if you ladies had heard anything about the pup I found?"

"We haven't heard a thing." Vicki's hands stilled on the material she handled, and Charlene stayed silent. She had other things she wanted to talk about, but that subject could go first.

"I asked at church on Sunday, and I was on the phone with Mrs. Palmer for an hour, talking about people we knew with dogs, but no one with a description like the one you found, and no one is missing any."

"Wonder how long I should wait until I assume that whoever lost her doesn't want her?" Silas mused.

Charlene liked that.

He was considerate of others but had a soft heart. And loved animals. Pretty much the perfect man. As long as he was considerate to his lady, which after what she'd heard what Silas had done for the last week, staying in Gladys LeFrak's house, she figured he was considerate all right.

"If someone hasn't come forward to claim that puppy by now, I don't think anyone's going to, but I'd give it another week." Kathy's words were serious, but she still had that blinking thing going on with Silas. Although... Charlene pushed her glasses farther up her nose. Maybe Kathy just had something in her eye. She couldn't tell from here.

Silas nodded. "All right. I figured I need at least two weeks, maybe a month. I hated to name her before we knew for sure that we were going to keep her, but it's hard to keep calling her that puppy."

"Once you fall in love with her, it's gonna break your heart to have someone come and take her," Vicki said, her eyes sad, like she'd had that happen to her.

"She's been a blessing to Gladys but even more to Mabel. She loves animals, and they've never had a dog before."

"You mean the girl's going to be a vet, and they've never had a dog?" Charlene couldn't help but ask.

Silas shook his head.

"I hope no one claims her then, because every kid should have a dog," Vicki said with finality.

"And every woman should have a handsome cowboy who will kiss her when her parents die," Teresa said, like the dam had broken and the words rushed out of her mouth like floodwater.

Charlene couldn't help but snort, grateful that she hadn't picked up her cup of coffee like she'd been tempted to. She'd have sprayed all over Silas. She was annoyed, but it was hard to stay annoyed with Teresa when she knew her heart was gold, she just...had never quite caught on to being a human and not a robot.

Charlene didn't know how else to describe it.

Silas's brows had raised up to his hairline, and now he was the one who looked like he had something in his eye.

"What Teresa is trying to say," Charlene began.

Teresa interrupted her. "Is that Gladys might move away, but if you kiss her, she might fall in love with you, so you need to do it like right now." Her words came out fast, like bullets out of a machine gun.

That's kind of the way they hit Silas too, and Charlene was surprised his body wasn't jerking. But his mouth hung open, and his chest moved unsteadily, like he was having trouble catching his breath.

Normally Charlene thought fast on her feet, but she wasn't quite sure she could salvage this situation. Men did not like to be told what to do, and Silas was most definitely a man.

His brows furrowed as he closed his mouth, and he seemed to have forgotten that anyone else was in the room as he took two long strides toward Teresa, bending down a little and saying low to her, "That would work? Kissing her?"

Teresa nodded. "If you do it right."

Silas dragged in a breath. "How do I do it right?"

Charlene gave herself a millisecond to get over her shock that not only did he not balk at the idea, but he wanted to know how to do it right.

She hustled over and inserted herself between Silas and Teresa. There was no way she was going to allow Teresa to tell Silas how to kiss someone. It would be the most robotic kiss in the history of the world.

"You have to be gentle," she began, taking Silas's arm and leading him carefully away from Teresa. Her job was most definitely done. "You want to make sure she knows you're focused only on her, so you can't be looking around at the scenery," Charlene said, giving him her best schoolmarm tone.

"No sightseeing during kissing. Got it," Silas said.

"You might want to get your phone and take notes," Vicki said. "If you have to ask how to kiss right, there's a list, and you need to be perfect the first time, because if Gladys is leaving, you might not get a second chance."

"Are you serious?" Silas asked, pulling his gaze away from Charlene's and lifting his brows at Vicki.

"A girl can tell a lot about a man from his kiss," Charlene said, feeling like that was something obvious to a woman but might not be so obvious to a man.

"She can? Like what?" Silas asked, and he seemed a bit like a mouse at a cat daycare.

"Like what he had for supper for one," Teresa said, having stood and now leaning over Charlene's shoulder.

"Thanks, Teresa. I'll take care of this. I've kissed more men than the rest of you combined." She wasn't sure whether that was true or not, but she didn't want Silas to have any doubts as to her experience. "Now, you need to be gentle, although it's not really the technique that's important."

"What?" Vicki asked, shock and almost outrage in her voice.

"It's not. It's how she *feels*. It's how you make her *feel*."

"Oh. Yeah. That's true," Vicki said, settling back down. "Carry on."

"How I make her feel?" Silas asked, like they had been talking in a different language, and he was having trouble following the conversation.

"Yes. A kiss is all about how you make her feel. A lot of times, men think a kiss is all about them. Them being macho or them being a Romeo. Or what's coming after." Charlene winked at Silas. He still had a befuddled look on his face and didn't even respond.

"So I want to make her enjoy the kiss, right?"

"Well, you don't want to slobber on her. But it's less about her enjoying the kiss or your skill at kissing and more about making her feel cherished. Like she's important to you. Like she's your whole world. You want to use endearments and stroke her face, like her skin is the sweetest thing you've ever touched, and stare at her like there's nothing else in the world you'd rather be looking at, and tell her how she makes you feel. Then, don't rush anything. It takes a lot of confidence to go slow, and girls like that. Plus, if you're going slow, she'll think you're enjoying it."

Silas was quiet for a moment, then he said, "So, treat her like an antique and not a sports car?"

Charlene's shoulders slumped. She'd been so hopeful. He'd been listening so intently. She thought she was getting somewhere with him.

"Yes! Yes! That's exactly right. An antique. Treat her like she's an antique. That's what women want."

Charlene didn't even bother to say anything to Teresa. There was no way this could have turned into a bigger disaster.

But that attitude only lasted for a couple of seconds. Charlene was a lot of things but never a quitter.

"No," she said firmly. "You don't want to treat her like an antique. That's a piece of junk. We're not talking about cars anyway."

"Wait. Teresa has a valid point. You take a lot of time, put a lot of effort and a lot of money into fixing an antique up. Run your rag over the paint, careful not to scratch it. Because you love it, because you care about it, because you want to get out and show it off to the world. Enjoy it. Have a Sunday drive, spend time with it. That's exactly what you want to do with your girl." Vicki shook her head. "Teresa, you are brilliant."

Well, when she put it like that, Charlene had to say she could get on board. If that's the way she had to talk to Silas to get him to understand, she'd do it. She should have figured that out from the beginning. After all, he was a motor guy.

It made her think of an analogy of her own.

"When you're building a motor, putting it together, you don't just drop the pieces in. You do it carefully, painstakingly, you can't rush it, because it has to be just right. That's how you want to kiss her."

Silas was nodding now, a thoughtful look on his face. Goodness, at her age she would have thought she couldn't learn anything new, but this was definitely the first time she'd compared kissing a girl to working on a car engine.

This was one matchmaking event that might not work out. Bringing cars into it. Nuts.

Chapter Fourteen

Give, take, forgive but most importantly, put God in the center. A marriage should be a contest to see who could treat the other the best.
- Linda Riggins, Central SC

"Your parents have nothing. They were in the process of trying to sell everything, which was why they moved here."

Gladys sat in stunned silence. The accountant watched her dispassionately. There was no reason for him to care, although maybe he was being unemotional because he wasn't used to delivering such terrible news to people.

Whatever it was, she needed a few minutes to catch her breath.

This was not what she was expecting to hear today.

Her concerns had been more about who was going to take her father's place, since she knew nothing about the company. She had no illusions about being able to run it herself, and she had been going to ask how she could sell it, if there was an easy way of moving someone into her father's spot.

"He has an offer on your place in LA, that sale is supposed to go through a week from tomorrow. The money from that should be enough to pay most of the debt of the business, so you won't have to declare bankruptcy, but he's already let all of the employees go and taken steps to close everything down."

Gladys shook her head, trying to make his words make sense. She didn't know anything about businesses in general, and she didn't know what steps needed to be taken to close a business.

"What was he going to do?" she asked, still reeling that the life they had was just an illusion.

"That's what he and your mother were flying to the Cities for. He had several offers on the table from businessmen looking for CEOs, and he'd considered a career in politics. All very hush-hush because no one knew what terrible financial straits the company was in. You won't be totally destitute. There's a fund for your sister's education, and that hasn't been touched. And there is an inheritance from your grandmother that you get when you're twenty-five."

"If I'm married," she mumbled.

"That's right." He didn't seem the slightest bit concerned about it.

"So, basically I'm destitute unless I get married?" It was a rhetorical question. That was what he had just said, but there was some small part of her that hoped that there was something...

"The house that you're living in now, here, is paid for. I think destitute might be a little bit of an exaggeration." He raised his brows. "We can continue on with what your dad started, selling the business and liquidating everything, or if you have any better ideas?"

"No. I went to school to be a counselor, I have no idea how to run the business, and if Dad couldn't do it, there's no way I could do anything better."

That was for sure. As much as her risk-taking personality sat in the back of her head saying go ahead and give it a shot.

They talked for a little while longer, with her accountant going through the details that would have to be done, the time she would have to be there as her father's heir to sign different things. And those kinds of things. She tried to pay attention, but in the back of her head, she was thinking there was no place in North Dakota for her to get a job with her counseling degrees. She'd have to go back to LA.

Or somewhere else. Somewhere she could start her own counseling business or, most likely, join with another group.

After the accountant left, she closed the door and leaned against it, discouraged.

She wanted to talk to Silas. It seemed like whatever was happening in her life, he could calm her, show her an angle she missed, and she loved that. But she'd used him so much, and she hadn't given anything back. She hated to go to him again.

Plus, she was an adult, and she had to learn to stand on her own two feet.

She wasn't hungry, but she walked slowly to the kitchen where the housekeeper had fruit and bagels set out for breakfast.

She supposed she should tell Kayla she needed to find another position. And then she'd need to learn to cook. Lovely.

Grabbing a pear, she walked out to the back porch and stood in the North Dakota sunshine, hot and bright, seeping into her skin and warming her soul.

What was the old saying about God never closed a door but he opened a window?

Things couldn't look as bleak as they felt. There had to be something, some way that she could pull things together and make it through.

Without leaving North Dakota.

Funny how when she first came, it had seemed barren and inhospitable and completely unpopulated, and now, the land had grown on her. The people.

Silas.

It was friendly and unpretentious and put her in mind of the place where she wanted to put roots and grow.

She'd taken two bites of her pear when her phone rang.

She pulled it out of her pocket, glancing at the screen. James Butler. The name seemed vaguely familiar.

"Hello?" she said, answering after she swallowed.

"Hello, is this Gladys?"

"Yes?"

"This is James Butler. I... I wanted to offer my condolences on the loss of your parents."

"Thank you." That couldn't have been the only reason he called, so she waited, racking her brain trying to remember where she heard the name and what he did.

"I worked with your father, he mentioned you a lot."

"Nice." So that was where she'd heard his name.

"My business partner and I were supposed to visit North Dakota with your dad last week. We were going to stay at his house for a few days. I don't know if he talked about that?"

She realized then that James and his business partner Hunter were the two men that her mother had planned for her to eat with the weekend after they were killed.

Gladys had forgotten all about it, but the men must have known what happened, since her parents were flying out and they would be meeting up to attend the meetings together.

"Yes. I remember now. You were supposed to come along with Hunter, and I was going to meet you at supper on Saturday night. The funeral and everything else just totally threw it out of my mind."

Leaning against the door, she tilted her head back, looking at the porch roof. The whole point of that meal, at least from her mother's perspective, was for Gladys to meet the two men to see if she would be interested in them, since her twenty-fifth birthday was approaching and her mom wanted her married.

Funny how such a short time could change her perspective, because at that point, she hadn't been the slightest bit interested in her inheritance and didn't care if she lost it.

She stood there thinking about her mother. She must have known that the money was drying up, the business was failing, and Gladys needed to marry. It could be that instead of seeing her mother as a pushy, overbearing woman who was only concerned about money and prestige, maybe her mom was setting her up with these men because she cared about her and wanted her to be financially secure, even as her mom and her dad were losing their business and their livelihood.

"Gladys?" James's voice came over the phone.

"Yeah. I'm still here. I'm sorry, it just brought back some memories."

"I'm sorry about that." He cleared his throat. "How's your sister holding up?"

Gladys blinked. Hadn't the dinner been about her? Her prospects? Her sister had an inheritance too, though. Maybe they'd been inviting them hoping at least one of them would hit it off.

"She's doing okay. A friend from the area found a stray puppy, and she's been taking care of her. She's studying to be a veterinarian and has never been allowed to have animals, so that's really been a blessing to her." Silas had loved that puppy. And yet, he hadn't even blinked when giving her to Mabel would help her. He gave her easily.

"I was hoping that maybe I could still come. I mean, I don't have any business out there anymore now that your father's not there, but... I wouldn't mind meeting the two of you."

Did he know about the inheritance? Was he still interested because he thought he'd end up being a millionaire?

Gladys had half a mind to ask him, but she didn't want to be rude. If he were attending the business meetings with her parents, then he might know her parents' financial situation or at least that they were looking for employment outside of their business. So he would know that much at least, and if he didn't know about the inheritance, then he might be interested just for the sake of interest. Which seemed far-fetched to Gladys. There were plenty of girls in the city. He wouldn't need to travel to a small town in North Dakota just to meet two.

The question about her sister seemed to be telling.

Maybe she was making a wrong decision, but her sister wasn't interested in men, since she wanted to finish her schooling.

And Gladys wasn't interested either. Sure, marrying would enable her to inherit her grandmother's money, but she didn't want to be stuck married to someone she didn't really like.

And divorce was not an option. Once she gave her word, when she made a vow, she intended to keep it. Silas had convinced her of that after their brief conversation on the subject.

"Thanks so much for calling and asking, but at this time, we're just trying to get over losing our parents and putting the pieces back together. Neither one of us are really up for company." It wasn't a lie, and it wasn't really an excuse, either. She definitely didn't feel like meeting a new suitor, and she knew Mabel didn't either, although Mabel was never interested in people.

"Okay," the man said after a slow pause. "If it's okay, I'll keep your number, maybe give you a call in a few months."

"That's fine," Gladys said, figuring it wouldn't hurt anything.

They hung up, and Gladys checked her phone since there had been a call she'd missed while she had been talking to James.

It was Charlene, one of the Piece Makers in town.

She left a voicemail, so Gladys pushed off the door, tossing the core of her pear as far out into the yard as she could, and clicked the button to listen to Charlene's message.

"Gladys, it's Charlene, with the Piece Makers in Sweet Water. We have quilts for you and your sister, I was wondering if you could come pick them up today? We'll be here at the church basement until five. Or if another day would suit better, you can give me a call and let me know. Thanks. Goodbye."

Gladys turned and walked in the house. She had things she needed to do, things the accountant had suggested, and a list he had given her, but for now, she was going to jump at the chance to get away from all that, take her mind off of it. Maybe she just wanted someone to talk to. The ladies in town wouldn't be able to give her any advice about her business, but she knew they would listen to her, and maybe that would be enough.

Plus, while she was in town, she'd stop at the garage. And see Silas.

The thought gave her the first glimpse of happiness she'd had since meeting the accountant. And she hurried even faster. Maybe they could eat a late lunch together.

Less than half an hour later, she pulled into the church. Mabel and she already had plenty of blankets for their beds, but she couldn't tell the Piece Makers that when they had taken the time to make quilts just for them.

The idea of seeing Silas along with the beautiful, sunny day almost had her smiling again as she grabbed a hold of the door, opening it and walking into the basement.

"Gladys! We're so glad you could make it," Charlene said, rising from her spot in the corner where she'd been cutting fabric.

"I'm sorry. You don't have to get up."

"I'm just excited for you to see the quilts."

"All of us are," Vicki said, moving from the quilting frame she'd been standing at. Kathy and Teresa were already at the table where a big box sat and where Charlene led Gladys.

"How are you doing?" Charlene asked, true concern on her face.

Gladys almost preferred the perfunctory "how are you doing?" versus the truly concerned "how are you doing?" If it were just a surface question, she could give a surface answer. But when someone truly asked like they truly cared, she hated not answering them with the truth. Or at least trying to figure out what the truth was. Because half the time, she wasn't even sure how she was doing.

"I guess I feel like I'm floating. Or sinking. Or just not in control of my life right now," she said honestly, voicing the thought that had been on her brain. The accountant's news had buffeted her like a storm tossed a boat around. It just felt like one more thing that hit her in her life.

"Oh, honey. It's so hard," Charlene said, wrapping her arms around Gladys and pulling her close.

It felt so good. Just to be held and comforted. Not to be told what she needed to do, or the problems she needed to fix, or be given advice or commands, but just comfort. She resisted the urge to burrow down into Charlene's arms like she was a small child being comforted by her mother and just hugged her back.

The other ladies gathered round, squeezing her and patting her on the shoulder.

This was definitely something that wouldn't have happened in LA, and the rather nebulous thought that maybe she might want to stay in Sweet Water began to solidify even more in her head. She'd been reluctant to sell the house, reluctant to think about moving anywhere else, and dreading the idea that there would be no work around here for her and she wouldn't have a choice. And this was partly why.

These ladies barely knew her, and yet they felt like friends.

She had the feeling that she could ask them for anything, and if it were in their power, they would give it to her, without expecting anything in return.

It wasn't exactly the culture she'd grown up in, but it was the kind of person she wanted to become. Like Silas.

Who would just be beside someone, supporting them, whenever they needed it.

Like these ladies, who seemed like they loved her no matter what she was.

She felt so much better when she finally stepped away, all four ladies smiling at her, a little sadly but with love.

Chapter Fifteen

Aside from God, I would say that what makes a marriage last is really listening to one another. A lot of things can be worked out by truly listening to the other person. Communication is usually heavy on talk and lighter on listening. I think it should be opposite. Thanks.
- Misty from Kansas

"I know you've heard this over and over, but it's true. Time heals. You'll get your footing again. Life will straighten out." Vicki had held onto her hand as she pulled away, and she patted it now.

"I think what you need is a diversion," Charlene said, sympathy lacing every word.

Gladys's ears perked up. A diversion was a great idea. Not something that would cause her to ignore her troubles, but something that she could put her brainpower into and focus on so that when she was overwhelmed with everything else she had to deal with, she would have something to think about.

"I'm listening," she said, not bothering to disguise the hope in her eyes. Maybe some people might like to sit in a corner and mourn. Mabel might be like that, where she just wanted to be by herself, just wanted to process things slowly, but that wasn't Gladys. Had never been. She would be much happier with a project. Something she could throw herself into.

"Oh, honey, I don't think you want to take on anything right now. You've just lost your parents. Go ahead and adjust to that, and just allow yourself time to grieve," Teresa said, her hand on Gladys's shoulder, her words sincere.

"I do better when I'm active. If I have a cause, a project, something to take my mind off things I need to deal with at home. That would be so nice."

"Well, if you're sure," Charlene said quickly before Teresa had a chance to let the words come out of her open mouth. "I wouldn't want you to do anything you're not ready for."

Gladys started to shake her head and say that she was ready, at least for a diversion, but Charlene saw something in her eyes that must have been agreement and didn't need words because she started again very quickly. "We've been thinking about something that you might be able to help us with."

"Help you?" Gladys asked, surprised. She thought they were going to tell her that she should pick up dog poop in the park or something. She didn't know. Maybe help someone in town. Volunteer at a homeless shelter, although there weren't many homeless shelters in Sweet Water. Maybe in Rockerton.

"What can I help you with?" These ladies had been so sweet to her, so wonderful at the funeral, and so kind now. She'd love to give back a little.

"Well," Charlene said, and it looked like there might have been a little bit of deviousness in her eyes, but Gladys shook that thought out of her head, because that couldn't be. "The Piece Makers have been doing something on the side, I mean, you know. We give quilts to people, and we try to do good in the town and in our little corner of the world, and one of those things we do is we match lonely people—"

"We're matchmakers. Like Cupid. That's us," Teresa said, interrupting Charlene and just getting straight to the point.

Maybe she could have used Charlene's more gentle way of breaking it, because as Gladys looked around at the sincere faces, she had a hard time imagining them being able to set two people up to fall in love successfully.

"We had a rather bad track record and a rather epic fail." Charlene paused delicately, as though the epic fail were something that she should have heard about.

Gladys hadn't, and she kind of shrugged her shoulders.

"And while we've had a bit of success in recent months, in the last year, we have someone that is presenting a bit of a challenge to us, and we were hoping you could help us."

"Sure. I mean, I don't really know a whole lot of people in the area, but if you need me to come up with names—"

"No. Nothing like that," Vicki said immediately.

"Oh." She wasn't sure exactly what else the ladies might think she could do. She supposed she had counseling skills, but...would that be something matchmakers could somehow use? She couldn't be unethical.

Using her skills as a counselor to manipulate someone into doing something definitely would hit the buttons for being unethical.

"We have a man, he's great, upstanding, bright, very responsible, would make a great husband and father," Vicki began.

"He sounds perfect," Gladys said, her words surface only, since the man sounded a lot like Silas, and that got her to thinking about him and about talking to him later, and it made her eager to leave.

"But he's lacking some of the skills that women need." Kathy said this very delicately.

"Skills?" Gladys asked, only half paying attention. Maybe they meant like cooking or something. "There's really nothing that a man can't learn. I mean, if you need me to teach him to scrub toilets or something..." She probably wouldn't be the best person to teach him that either. Her family had a maid all her life. Although, come on, how hard can it be?

"We want you to teach him how to kiss."

After Charlene spoke, the church was silent.

Gladys was no longer thinking about Silas. Her entire focus was on the sweet ladies in front of her.

"You want me to teach him how to kiss?" she asked, hoping she'd heard them wrong. But she couldn't think of anything that rhymed with kiss that had to do with housework or relationships in general.

"Yes. He's perfect in every other way, but he really doesn't understand what a woman is looking for when a man kisses her, and we figured since you were from LA..." Vicki let her sentence trail off, and Gladys had to smile at the idea that people from LA might have more experience in these kinds of things than someone from North Dakota.

It was a bias, but an accurate one most likely.

Still, while she'd kissed plenty of guys, she wasn't real thrilled about the idea. "I could give him some suggestions, but you're not actually talking about real kissing?"

The ladies seemed so sweet and harmless, but the idea of kissing someone she didn't know or like seemed...a little much, even for her.

Maybe before she met Silas, she might have done it without a second thought, but somehow at this moment, it didn't sit quite right. Still, she couldn't tell the ladies no.

"We actually were. Pointers are great, but his technique needs some work." Charlene shook her head sadly.

If it had been anyone else, Gladys would wonder if the sweet lady was manipulating her. But she just couldn't imagine these harmless ladies, sitting in the basement of the church spending their free time quilting for the less fortunate, would do something so devious.

"Okay. I... I think I can do that." She didn't want to. But again, she just couldn't say no. Not after everything they'd done for her. Not if she could help them in any way. "Are you going to give me his number? Or how do I get in touch with him?"

"Actually, we talked to Silas earlier today, and his dad and brothers went to an auction south of Rockerton, and he's holding the garage down by himself. But he'll be free at lunchtime." Charlene looked at her watch. "So you could probably grab some lunch and take it to him, and you guys could have your first lesson then, unless you feel like you need to do some research first?" Charlene asked, like the idea was preposterous that Gladys would need to do any kind of preparation in order to teach someone how to kiss.

Not that Gladys was paying attention. They wanted her to teach Silas how to kiss?

Well, that was...unexpected.

Then another thought occurred to her.

"Who are you setting him up with?" she asked, interrupting Teresa saying something about not putting onions on their sandwiches if they were going to practice kissing after lunch.

"Oh, we have someone in mind, but so far, we haven't been successful in our efforts, but I'm sure you'll find out with the rest of the town when we are," Charlene said airily, waving her hand in the air, her blue hair bobbing just a bit as she turned.

"I'm sure you're busy, and we don't want to hold you up anymore, although if you need us, we're here and you can come and talk to us anytime," she said over her shoulder as she walked away.

That seemed abrupt.

But maybe they were just uncomfortable talking about their matchmaking efforts. That had to be it. If word got out that they were trying to match her up with someone, she would balk at it. Every other single person in town was probably the same. No one wanted to have a bunch of old ladies, no matter how sweet and kind they were, manipulating their lives.

Silas. On one hand, the idea of kissing him... Had she ever thought about kissing him? There had always been an attraction she felt, but it hadn't been something she ever thought she'd act on. He was just...too different, too straight, too not her type.

Except, maybe he was. Not because he had changed, but because she had.

She couldn't admit it to anyone, but the idea of kissing him sent a thrill of sparks down her spine, and rather than dreading it, like she thought she would do, she was actually relishing the idea.

In fact, there was something very appealing about the idea of being in control, telling him to follow her lead, and showing him something so intimate yet simple.

"Wait!" Teresa said, stopping Gladys as she walked toward the door. "We forgot to show you your quilts!"

"She can come back for them after lunch," Charlene said quickly. "That way, she can let us know how the kissing lesson went."

Charlene didn't rub her hands together, but Gladys got the feeling she really wanted to.

The mention of the quilts reminded her of her parents and of all of her problems, and she stopped and turned.

"Thank you, ladies. I appreciate having this to take my mind off everything else."

It would be a great distraction. She actually felt excited about something for the first time since her parents died.

Not that she wasn't still sad, and not that she wasn't still grieving, but she had something to look forward to, along with all the crushing weight of responsibility and grief and hard decisions.

The Piece Makers were lifesavers.

Chapter Sixteen

Besides the obvious reason of love, honesty is imperative,. Honesty gives all that goes on a foundation.
- Shirley A. Strait from Mississippi

Silas wiped off his wrench and set it carefully back in his toolbox. Part of his job was to keep his tools clean and neat. So that when he needed them, he was able to find them easily. There was nothing more frustrating than to be dealing with a difficult job and not be able to find the tools he needed to work.

"Hey there."

He lifted his head at the familiar voice.

"Hey." He closed the door of his tool chest and shoved the rag in his pocket. "You're like a stray dog that comes around when it's suppertime looking for scraps?" he asked, teasing her a little, hoping she was okay with it.

"I think it's more like you being the stray dog, since I have the food." She held up a bag that he recognized as being from Patty's Diner.

"I hope those are hamburgers."

"And French fries, which hopefully are still hot, but we gotta get to them."

"I just need to wash my hands. Good thing my brothers aren't here, or we might have to share all that."

"I stopped in to see the Piece Makers, and they told me that your family was at an auction, and you were here by yourself." She looked a little nervous, and he wondered why that would bother her.

It wasn't like she'd never been alone with him before, like they didn't spend the last week or so sleeping on couches together.

It must have been something else, or maybe it was just a passing thought about her parents.

"Been having a good day?" he asked as he walked to the sink, turning the water on and using the rough soap on his hands.

"It's been really good. After starting out really bad."

"Bad?" He turned concerned eyes on her. "Did the meeting with your accountant not go well?" That was where she was going when they parted earlier.

"Not well is probably a really positive way to look at it." She didn't leave him hanging but continued. "My dad was in the process of selling the business because it was completely bankrupt. In fact, it was in the red. Basically, my accountant said I have nothing, although Mabel still has her college fund, so that's taken care of, and the house here in North Dakota is paid for, so I have some equity there if everything is a wash in the business."

She spoke dispassionately, and it didn't surprise him that she divulged so much. After all, they'd definitely grown closer over the last week or so. He wasn't sure where he stood in her eyes, but for him, he considered her a good friend.

"That was unexpected." He shut the water off after rinsing his arms and hands and grabbed a towel to dry them. "You seem like you're taking it okay. Or has it not quite hit you yet?" Maybe he should offer words of sympathy. Something to comfort, commiserate. He didn't know. He wasn't any good with emotions, but he must not have done anything too terrible, because she shook her head.

"It was a shock, and I admit to spending a few spaced-out minutes in the meeting, just trying to figure out what in the world I was going to do, but I have a feeling that everything will work out."

He thought of her inheritance and wondered where that would play a part. For some reason, the idea that she would be stepping up her efforts to find a husband did not sit well with him.

"Because of your inheritance?" He meant it to be a statement, but his voice lifted on the last syllable, like he was asking.

"Not long after I got out of the meeting with the accountant, I got a call from one of the men who were supposed to be eating with us the Saturday after my parents were killed."

She paused, her mouth open like she was trying to figure out how to phrase something; maybe she hadn't figured out what she wanted to say in her own mind yet.

"I thought my mom was being pushy by trying to shove men down my throat and getting me married off, and I didn't really care about the inheritance. But in hindsight, I wonder if she was doing it because she knew the state of the business and the fact that they weren't going to have any money, and I was going to need it."

Silas was quiet for a moment, just standing there in the garage, thinking. Finally he said, "Maybe if that was her intention, she should have just come out and said something to you. You're an adult. You have a postgraduate degree. Why was she treating you like a child by manipulating things behind your back, when she could have just had a mature conversation with you and given you the choice?"

"I wondered that, too."

"I don't mean to talk your mom down; maybe she just had your best interest at heart. Sometimes, when we know our back's against the wall and we have to make a decision, we end up making the wrong one."

"That's true, but when we have someone pushing us in a direction we don't want to go, we have a tendency to push back rather than looking at it with objective eyes." She lifted her shoulder. "I guess I'll never know, but if Mom knew, if that's what she was doing, trying to push me toward someone, I wish we could have talked about it."

"I'm not always the best at talking about things, but it seems like you avoid a lot of misunderstanding, and even more hurt feelings and contention, if you just speak up."

Her eyes opened wide, and she swallowed, almost like she were guilty of something.

His eyes narrowed.

"Do you have something you want to tell me?" he asked as they walked together toward the man door. It was a beautiful day outside, and neither of them had said anything, but he assumed they'd be eating outside. They didn't have the table set up or anything, but they had a few folding chairs set out behind the garage.

"Well, maybe."

Something in her tone made him shift the cold bottles of water he grabbed from the cooler. Maybe he was a little guilty too. Since the Piece Makers had asked him to kiss her to take her mind off her troubles, and he had no intention of telling her that.

Maybe he should.

Chapter Seventeen

Trust and good communication.
- Theresa Palmieri from California

Gladys followed Silas out of the garage to the chairs that were set up. It would be kind of hard to teach him how to kiss if they were sitting down side by side, but she wasn't sure how to broach the subject, so she sat, hoping for an opening that wouldn't be too awkward.

Silas prayed for their food, then she opened it and gave them each a sandwich while he put her drink in the cup holder on the armrest of her chair.

They talked about the weather and the quilts that the Piece Makers had made but had been overshadowed, by far, with the request the Piece Makers had made.

"You seem a little distracted. Are you okay?" Silas's face showed concern as he finished the last of the sandwich.

She almost smiled because she had done what Teresa had said and asked for the sandwiches with no onions.

But then, as his concern permeated her brain, she remembered that she wasn't supposed to be happy. She was supposed to be sad. She was an orphan. Her parents were gone. She had the weight of the world on her shoulders while she tried to figure out what to do with the mess that was left.

To her consternation, her eyes filled with tears.

"You're not okay," Silas said, putting his hand on her arm and leaning closer.

She fought the tears, determined not to cry. She'd already cried more than she ever thought she could and definitely more than she thought she would at losing her parents. Just... She supposed the old saying about you don't know what you have until it's gone was true in her case.

Even if she wasn't that close to them, she hadn't realized how much a person's parents influenced their everyday life, even when they weren't specifically thinking about them.

The Piece Makers were right. She needed to get her mind off of it, and they had provided the perfect distraction.

"I'm fine. Just, every once in a while, the oddest thing will trigger a memory, or thought, or remind me that life isn't the same as what it used to be, and my eyes just fill."

"There's no shame in crying. It's a natural reaction."

"I know. I just keep doing it. And it might be a natural reaction, but it shows weakness."

"I don't know about that. The Bible talks about God seeing our tears. He's moved by them. He seems to want to see them and judges us sincere when He does."

There he was again, spouting wisdom that she had no idea about. "I didn't know that was in the Bible."

"Thou tellest my wanderings: put thou my tears into thy bottle: are they not in thy book?"

Gladys sat stunned. It was true. God really did care about her tears. "Does that mean I shouldn't try to stop my crying anymore?"

Silas's smile was gentle, and she stared at it for just a bit. Not just because it made her feel cherished somehow, but because of the way the one side of his mouth kicked up and his eyes crinkled and he looked boyish and handsome and her heart fluttered in a way that was not uncomfortable.

"I don't know that you should go around crying crocodile tears all the time, I just wanted you to know that it doesn't always have to be a struggle to hide them. At least not in God's eyes, and that's really the only thing that matters, isn't it?"

She found herself nodding before she even thought about whether or not she agreed. She supposed he was right. God's opinion really was the only opinion that mattered, but it was so hard to remember that as she lived her daily life. Especially since she'd been raised that appearances matter, and it was what people thought of a person that was the most important thing. And she didn't want to do anything that would offend anyone or that would lower their opinion of her. Even if it all was just a show.

She wished her parents hadn't been into the show so much and that they had been more honest with her about the situation with the business. Sure, she'd been busy getting her postgraduate degree, but surely she could have done something.

She would have helped in the business or at least been someone to share the burdens with, because surely they'd been under an enormous amount of pressure.

It was all too late, but Silas's words brought it back. Putting on a show just so people would think certain things of her, especially if those things weren't true, was pointless and wrong.

"What?" Silas said, still grinning a little, although his eyes were dark with concern.

"I was just thinking. Not crying is almost like putting on a show, isn't it?"

His brows went up, and he tilted his head a little before he said, "I guess. Maybe. Although it might be consideration for other people who are uncomfortable with tears. Or it might just be the fact that you don't want to draw attention to yourself. Or at least what you perceive is probably negative attention." He thought about it a little bit more. "I guess I'm not tempted to cry that often, but if I were, and if I fought it, you're probably right. I wouldn't want people to see me as weak, so I guess that is a show."

That didn't help her staring problem at all. Now her mouth hung open, and she barely realized it.

He seemed so wise and so confident, yet he just admitted that he had faults too. Which, in her experience, was pretty unusual for a man, any man, to do.

"From your reaction, I want to just point out that I'm vulnerable here. Because people don't expect men to cry. I assume you're looking at me like that because you wouldn't think the idea would even cross my mind."

It took her a second to absorb what he was saying, because she'd been so caught up in thinking about character and integrity and honesty and how he seemed to have them all, and wasn't afraid to admit the truth, even when the truth wasn't flattering.

"No. Not at all. I was actually thinking pretty much the opposite. That it takes a certain type of man to be willing to admit weakness. And you don't think people admire that, that people should, but I do. You're honest, and you felt like being honest, even if it made you look bad, was more important than looking good. That's unusual, in my experience anyway, and I appreciate it."

She'd embarrassed him, because he kind of leaned back with a bemused look on his face and just shook his head a little. But he didn't argue with her because she was right. And he didn't say anything, which made her think that he was humble as well as honest.

Since they were talking about honesty, she figured that might be the best way to approach what the Piece Makers had suggested.

"When I went in to pick up my quilts at the Piece Makers, they thought it might be a good idea for me to do something to get my mind off of my parents and all of the pressure I'm under."

"I agree. Wise women."

"They said that they had someone they wanted to match up, because I guess they see themselves as somewhat of Sweet Water's matchmakers."

"Yeah. Sometimes with disastrous results, but yeah."

"And they wanted me to help them."

"Match people?"

"No. The... There's someone who is a really good person, and they want to see him find someone, but...he can't kiss."

"Ouch." The amusement in his eyes said that the idea of a bunch of older ladies telling someone they couldn't kiss was a real insult.

She bit her lip, because she didn't want him to find out that they had meant him. Maybe she should have done this a different way. Because if she was going to be honest, she was going to have to come out and tell him that *he* was the one she was supposed to teach to kiss.

"Go on," he prompted her when she hesitated.

She understood, always had, why it was so tempting to lie. After all, she didn't want to insult or embarrass him.

But a little lie was just as much of a sin as a big lie, even if it was meant to keep someone from getting their feelings hurt. Or to protect them from something. God never made any exclusions for lying.

It was wrong across the board.

She remembered learning that when she was little, but she kind of pushed it aside, thinking that her own wisdom was better than God's.

Probably, God knew that once a person was okay uttering little lies, big lies would slip off their tongues even easier.

She put her garbage in the bag and stood from her chair, walking over to the fuel tank that was sitting not far away, then turning around and leaning against it. Her arms crossed over her chest. Less for protection and more because she needed something to do with them, rather than just let them hang at her sides.

It was a testament to her nervousness.

"They wanted me to teach this person how to kiss."

He paused in the act of putting his own garbage in his bag and jerked up to look at her. "Like, give them instructions?"

"That's what I asked. But they pointed out I was from LA, and I think the insinuation was that I've probably kissed a lot of people and I shouldn't have a problem giving demonstrations if necessary."

"I guess I would have set them straight about that."

"I would have." She took a breath. "Then I found out who I was supposed to teach, and it didn't seem like such an onerous task anymore."

She hadn't been planning on saying that at all, but she hadn't expected the conversation to veer in this direction, either.

His face became impassive, and he jerked his chin to acknowledge her words but didn't say anything as he stood, taking the garbage and throwing it in the trash before walking over, one hand in his pocket, one hand behind his neck.

"I suppose they're right. That probably would take your mind off other things. In that sense of the word, it would be a good distraction." He looked like he was about to say more, then he paused, his brows drawn. "Who did they suggest needed practice kissing?"

"You."

He didn't move for several moments that felt long and drawn out and like they stretched into eternity, and then, rather than be offended like she had feared, his lips lifted just a little.

"I guess the ladies are probably right. I probably do need a little instruction."

She wasn't quite sure how to read that look on his face. It...looked amused and also like someone had gotten the better of him.

It was not the way she expected him to look, especially when she just admitted that people had said he needed to learn how to kiss, and maybe he was smiling because she said it wouldn't be a hard task for her.

Had she admitted too much?

She liked him, sure, and was definitely attracted to him, but they weren't really two people who would ever be able to be together.

They were too different.

He shoved his other hand in his pocket and tilted his head. "When were you thinking my instruction was going to begin?"

She had to admit he was a little intimidating. He wasn't upset like she expected, and he wasn't acting at all like she expected. And he certainly wasn't acting like someone who was insecure about his ability to kiss.

"Now?" she said, although it came out like a question, when she had meant to sound firm and confident.

He nodded his head. "I'm not saying I don't need to be taught, because I guess I probably do, and I'm not going to turn this down, but I have a confession to make."

His voice was low and a little rumbly, and she tried not to shiver, because he wasn't saying anything romantic, and she should be paying attention to his words, not going all mushy and tingly over his tone.

"Okay. I can't imagine it's anything too terrible." If there was ever a straight shooter, it was Silas. Whatever he was confessing wasn't going to be any big deal.

"I talked to the Piece Makers earlier today."

She nodded.

"They told me that you seemed overwhelmed by everything that's been happening to you and that I should try to take your mind off of it by...kissing you."

They stared at each other, and she was sure she was coming to the conclusion that he already had reached.

The Piece Makers called themselves matchmakers.

Silas and she were their latest project.

Chapter Eighteen

Keeping the door to communication open, listening to each other.
- Kay Zaugg from Utah

Silas wasn't sure what to think. Or what to do.

After all, he was mostly okay with kissing her to get her mind off of her problems. And because he wanted too.

But the idea that people were pushing them together rubbed him the wrong way. But he had to give them credit for their deviousness.

But he'd already decided that he couldn't kiss her if he didn't truly mean it from the depths of his soul, not without saying something to her.

He hadn't decided whether that depth of the soul feeling was there, or whether it was just something his flesh really wanted.

Because there was no doubt he wanted to kiss her.

But he had to give the matchmakers credit for creativity. Telling her that he needed instructions in kissing.

It was totally believable and probably true. So much he wanted to just laugh. Because none of the girls that he ever kissed had been overwhelmed with his abilities, and none of them had stuck around long.

He never thought to blame it on his technique, but maybe that was it.

Regardless, he wasn't against doing a little practicing. Although, he wouldn't have been interested with anyone else, and her comment that she wasn't interested until she found out it was him was something that stuck in his head.

He'd think about that stuff later. He didn't really want to focus on it right now, because it might lead to more than what he thought this was, which was not a game exactly, but fun nonetheless.

"So they told you that you need to kiss me. And they told me that I needed to teach you to kiss. That right?" she asked, tilting her head like she just couldn't believe it.

He nodded. "Looks that way. If you hadn't been honest about it, you might be giving me lessons right now, and neither one of us would know it."

She looked a little disappointed, or maybe that was his imagination, and she said softly, "Yeah."

So maybe he was being a little forward, and maybe he would regret this, but he didn't think about it too much before he said, "I'll still take those lessons. I laughed a little when you said that the Piece Makers thought I needed them, but then, thinking back, maybe I do."

"Women have complained about the way you kiss?" she asked, humor in her voice.

"I've never had any outright complaints, but I've never had anyone stick around too long either."

"Maybe that's because you're quiet, and they don't know what you're feeling, and also because you're pretty focused on cars and motors."

"So you're gonna give me some advice on my love life in general? And forget the kissing lessons?" Okay, maybe he was pushing a little hard, but then he'd been kind of getting into the idea of doing a little kissing, and he didn't want to give that up.

"Oh no, mister. You're getting lessons," she said, sounding for the first time in several weeks like the woman who'd been coming to his place at night and drag racing after midnight.

He couldn't keep his lips from turning up. "That sounds like the Gladys I know."

"You like the bossy part of me?" she asked, like maybe she'd gotten complaints over the years about her being too bossy or too commanding.

"I do. I like that you know what you want. I like that you're not afraid. I like that you're not afraid to push boundaries and test limits, because I feel like in order to live a true Christian life, you have to push back at a lot of things that are pushing against you. Someone who's not afraid to do that, who's not afraid to forge her own path, swim against the current, and doesn't get scared easily, will have what it takes to endure and even thrive in the Christian life."

She blinked and leaned back a little, like his words were unexpected, almost blindsiding her, but in a good way, he hoped. Since it meant she knew he was sincere.

"I like the variety in your personality as well. You have a postgraduate degree, and people wouldn't expect you to be out drag racing. Also, I know we really don't have social classes in our country anymore, but people like you don't usually hang out with people like me."

He paused for a minute there, hoping she took that right. He wasn't insulting her, and he wasn't knocking himself. But the fact of the matter was, blue-collar and white-collar typically only saw each other when they needed each other's services. They didn't understand their different lifestyles and the problems that went with them, and they didn't usually hang out together.

Her nod said she got it. So he went on. "I love that you're not afraid to do that. That you're not afraid to be friends with people who aren't exactly like you. That you don't think the things you do are the only good things in the world but have an appreciation for the fact that it takes us all to make the country run."

Her look was thoughtful. "You might be giving me a little bit too much credit. Definitely hanging out with you has opened my eyes, but sometimes I feel like I just use you. Because our relationship is so lopsided."

"That's okay. You can pay me back with the kissing lessons."

She laughed a little. "That's where you're supposed to say, 'That's not true. Our relationship is equal.'"

"I did. Or at least, I said it would be after you give me kissing lessons."

"You don't look the slightest bit insecure about your ability to kiss. I'm not sure whether to believe you or to think that maybe you're just trying to do what the Piece Makers said and distract me." She lifted her shoulder. "If that's what you're doing, it's working. I'm feeling lighter than I have in days."

"Now you're giving me credit that I don't deserve. Because, honestly, I'm just really getting into the whole idea of kissing you. Now that I've been thinking about it, the idea of not is disappointing."

He didn't want to be too serious because the Piece Makers had been absolutely right. Talking about kissing had totally gotten her mind off all the things she had to handle, and she looked less careworn, just from talking to him for these few minutes.

"I can't say that I've never taken the Piece Makers seriously, because I respect their age, and their wisdom as well, but I guess I never really took their matchmaking efforts seriously, or their thoughts on romance. Or maybe I should just say, when they asked me to kiss you to take your mind off your problems, I thought they were a little nuts. But you look happier than you have for days, and the Piece Makers are to thank for that."

"And you," she said easily. "You didn't have to listen to them, and you didn't have to care. Kissing is kind of a big request, but it would never work for just anyone to have done it. It had to be you."

They stood staring at each other. Silas with his throat dry and his heart hammering. She hadn't said he was the only one, and she hadn't indicated any interest in a relationship, but she seemed to insinuate that he was in a select group of men. And wasn't repulsive to her.

He found he wanted more, but he'd take that for now.

"I guess I feel the same. And maybe they knew it. That I wouldn't have been interested in taking just anyone's mind off their problems by kissing her, but I could definitely get on board with you."

Her face brightened with his words, and he wondered if maybe she was feeling the same way he was. That the friendship they had and the attraction he felt—although he didn't know whether she felt that too—seemed more and more like something they could build a relationship on.

He wouldn't call the Piece Makers divine messengers, but with everything that was moving into place, he almost felt like it was just one more sign that maybe Gladys wasn't as wrong for him as what he had originally thought.

"So, about those kissing lessons," she murmured, pushing off the tank she'd been leaning on and walking forward.

"I think lunch break is a good time to get started on kissing lessons," he said. Hoping she was meaning what he thought she was. And that they were going to start right now.

He'd barely thought that, and she had her mouth open to say something, when the crunch of gravel under tires floated over to them. Someone was pulling into the shop.

Her face fell. "It sounds like you're needed."

"Yeah. That won't be any of my family, since they're all at the auction." He really wanted to ignore the fact that someone was probably going to want him. He wanted to close the distance between them and continue with what they were doing.

Disappointment squeezed his chest, and rather than moving away, he put his hand on her cheek, cradling her face.

"So maybe no actual examples, but you can at least give me some instructions to think about."

He just wanted the kissing thoughts to stay in his brain. Because thinking about kissing Gladys was about the best thing he'd thought about in a long time.

She smiled. "Girls like it when you're interested and you show it." She put her hand over his. "When you touch them like you care. When you're gentle. When you're considerate of their feelings and don't try to kiss them for the first time in front of people."

She grinned a bit about that last comment, because maybe she knew that he was thinking he was *this close* to forgetting about the people who were at the garage and kissing her anyway.

"Gentle. Care. Show it. No audience." He dropped his hand. "I think I can remember all that."

They shared a look of amusement, but he was definitely feeling something a little deeper, stronger, than just mere amusement.

Something about her expression told him that maybe she was feeling it too.

"You're a quick study," she said. "I think this is going to be fun." She winked at him before she walked by him, through the door he had opened, and into the garage.

Yeah, he was pretty sure she was feeling it too. Bemused, he followed her and wasn't prepared to see his sister-in-law, Marigold, standing at the other end of the garage holding a baby in one arm and pushing the other one of her twins in a stroller.

Maybe it was the look on his face, or maybe it was something on Gladys's, because Marigold's look went from tired and hassled to speculative and amused.

"Am I interrupting something?" she asked, sounding a little snarky. In a good way.

For once, Gladys wasn't forging ahead but took smaller steps, uncertain.

"We're just finishing up lunch. You came at the perfect time. Although... You know no one's here?"

Her husband, Dodge, had gone to the auction as well. He couldn't imagine that Marigold didn't know.

"I was hoping that Sadie was here?" Her brows had drawn down, and she chewed on her lip.

"She went with the guys," Silas answered, coming to stand beside Gladys. Without thinking about it, he put his hand on her back, more for comfort, he supposed, than anything else.

"You know Gladys LeFrak." He barely waited for her nod. "Gladys, this is Marigold, my sister-in-law." He indicated the baby she held. "This is one of her twins. I have trouble telling them apart, but one is Jane and the other is Sally."

Marigold stepped forward with the hand that had been pushing the stroller outstretched. "I've seen you around and at the funeral. I'm so sorry for your loss."

While those words had been repeated over and over by tons of other people, Marigold truly seemed to mean them, and they didn't seem to strike any grieving note for Gladys, who smiled and easily reached for Marigold's hand.

Maybe it was just his imagination, but when she moved back, she seemed to move even closer to him, and without really planning it, his hand slipped around her waist.

"Thank you. I remember you, although it was a long day, capping off a long week, and I would never have remembered your name."

"It's okay. It's an odd name. That's why I gave my babies very common, very plain, very easy to remember names. Maybe they'll wish they had something fancy, but isn't that the way we are? We always want what we don't have." Marigold shrugged her shoulders, like she couldn't change the irony of life. "And, as a parent, that's what we're always trying to do for our children, give them what we didn't have."

Silas nodded along, although he supposed that was something he'd have to find out for himself, since he'd never really thought about it.

Under his arm, Gladys trembled a little, and immediately he remembered what she had said about certain things triggering memories that made her sad.

He also remembered what she said about hating to cry in front of people, not wanting to seem weak.

So, to keep the attention off of her, he said, "Did you need something from Sadie? Is there something I can do?"

Marigold bit her lip. "I really hate to ask, because I know you're here by yourself, but my sisters are all away, and my mom needs my help at the auction barn. It'll just be for a couple of hours, but I need someone to watch the kids."

The twins had been in the garage before, but Marigold or Dodge had always been with them. Silas enjoyed holding them, feeding them, and he'd even changed a diaper or two—with twins, there were a ton of diapers. But he'd never watched both of them at the same time by himself.

Still, he eyed the pudgy little baby in her arms and wondered to himself how hard could it be?

"It's fine. You can leave them here."

"I didn't want to ask you, because—"

"It's fine. That's what family's for," he said simply. She needed someone to help, and he could do it. There wasn't anything pressing in the garage, which was why all of his brothers felt like they could leave. He did have work he could do, but nothing that had a definite deadline.

Mostly, his presence was needed in case an emergency happened.

"What if you get called out?" Marigold chewed on her lip.

"I'll help him." Gladys spoke up from his side, and he tightened his hold on her. Maybe it was a bit of a hug, or maybe just a squeeze of reassurance. He could tell she wasn't trembling anymore, though. And he appreciated her support.

"Oh, I couldn't ask you to do that," Marigold started.

"You didn't. I volunteered. And it'll be fun."

"And if I have some kind of emergency, I'll give you a call, so you know, but Gladys will be here, and there's no rush to get back."

Marigold nodded. She knew that if a truck came in needing a repair, or if one broke down along the road, he'd need to go immediately. "All right. If you're sure. My mom was pretty desperate."

"We're sure. Go help your mom. I hate to see anything happen to her. It's dangerous to work cattle if you don't have enough people to help."

Marigold nodded again, the crease between her eyebrows the only sign that she worried about her mom. "I'd put Jane in the stroller with her sister, but she hates the stroller."

Silas reached out and took the chubby little girl from her mom.

He looked enough like his brother—her dad—that she usually didn't have too much trouble going to him even if he hadn't seen her in a while, although Marigold had just had them in the garage a few days ago.

"Dada! Dada!" the little girl said happily, taking both hands and slapping his short beard.

"She says that to everyone. It's the one word she knows," Marigold said in a conspiratorial voice to Gladys, almost as though she were afraid Gladys would think that Silas was Jane's actual dad.

"So she said 'Dada' first?" Gladys said with a sympathetic look.

"Yes, unfortunately. As much as I tried to get her to say 'Mama,' she insisted on 'Dada.' And this one," she nodded at Sally still in the stroller, "hasn't said anything yet. Both of them will hum, but neither of them gets the "ah" part out for Mama."

"Keep working on it. By the time they graduate high school, they'll probably know who you are," Silas said casually while rubbing his nose against Jane's and making her giggle.

"Nothing like a brother-in-law to make you feel like a competent mother." Marigold sighed wearily.

"If you find a woman who feels like a competent mother, I'd pay her to start lecturing the rest of us, because I've never heard anyone say they feel competent when it comes to motherhood," Silas murmured.

His comment made Gladys look at him like he'd grown a second head. He guessed she wasn't sure what someone like him would know about being a parent.

He shrugged. "I'm just repeating the stuff that people tell me."

She snorted out a laugh. "I doubt that, but that was a good comeback."

Marigold laughed along with them, then handed the baby bag over, along with another bag and an entire pack of diapers. "Maybe this is overkill, but I would always rather be prepared."

Silas appreciated that. He'd rather have too many diapers than have a mess and not be able to change the kid.

After she'd given them some instructions, then stopped and turned around and gave them more, and stopped once more with her hand on the knob and with her mouth open, Silas finally said, "Marigold. It's okay. I've got your number. If we have any questions, any at all, I'll call you. I promise."

Marigold looked at him for a moment, closed her mouth, looked at him again, nodded, and said, "Thank you."

She turned, pulling the door open and walking out.

She'd no sooner closed the door than Gladys laughed. "I'm not sure she trusts you," she said, laughter in her voice as she smiled at Jane, who was looking at her like she was trying to decide whether or not she was going to like this new person.

"You got that impression too?" he said, grinning.

"Well, you have to admit it's not normal for a mother to bring her children to a garage and drop them off, even if you are her brother-in-law." She tilted her head, a smile on her face as she made googly eyes at the baby, but then she gave him a look. "In fact, I'm kind of impressed. There are a lot of men who wouldn't have welcomed this interruption in their day."

Silas raised his eyebrows, acknowledging her words, but then he shook his head, as though shaking them off.

They turned together, Jane in his arms, and walked back to the stroller.

"I guess I just feel like whatever God puts in front of me, I'm going to do to the best of my ability. I mean, if she would have wanted me to do open heart surgery on them, I'd have had to pass."

"Thankfully."

"I think a lot of times we say no, either because we doubt ourselves or prefer not to have the hassle, rather than looking at each opportunity like it comes from the Lord. And then digging in and doing our best. Yes?"

She seemed to chew on that for a little bit. Jane gurgled, and she reached up and Jane grabbed her hand, wrapping her chubby little fingers around one of Gladys's and chortling.

"Maybe I shouldn't be so hasty to get rid of my dad's company? Maybe God put that in my lap for a reason?"

"Maybe. Or since your dad was already getting rid of it when you got it, maybe not."

"That's just it! How can you tell the difference?"

"Prayer? And it's always a good idea to get advice from people who are wiser and further along in their spiritual walk than you are."

"How about I just go ask advice from people who are going to say what I want them to?" Gladys said, being a little sarcastic but also seeming to acknowledge the truth in his words.

He laughed. "That's what most people do. I guess that's what we really want to do, because it's hard to give up what we want in favor of what we know is right. Although, the more often you do it, the easier it gets."

Jane leaned over, putting her arms out, including the one that was holding onto Gladys's thumb, toward Gladys, like she wanted to slip into Gladys's arms.

Gladys took her happily and cooed and made faces at her while Silas hunkered down to give Sally some attention.

After a few minutes, Gladys said, "Is it okay if I take them for a walk?"

"I think that would be great." He stood, looking down at her. "You want me to go with you?"

"No. I was actually thinking if I take them for a while, that'll get us out of your hair and you'll be able to get a few things done."

"If you want me to go back to work, just say so."

"Go back to work."

"Taskmaster."

They laughed, and she adjusted the girls with Jane on her hip and Sally in the stroller while Silas opened the door for her. "If you need me, text me or something. I'll keep an ear out."

She nodded as she left.

Chapter Nineteen

In our case, letting each other be their own person. We do almost everything together, but we also are fine with each other doing their own thing. We married later in life and this has worked really well for us.
- Mary Stalnaker from Alton, VA

"I'll be in my garage later if you want to come over," Silas said as Gladys got ready to leave.

They'd watched the twins for a couple of hours before Marigold came back for them. Then Gladys had hung out at the garage until his family had gotten back from the auction.

They were unloading the trucks, talking about taking a tow to haul back a wreck they'd bought.

Gladys really wanted to take him up on it. But she shook her head. "This has been an awesome day. Just what I needed. I totally had my mind off of everything that I've been thinking about the last week or so, and I feel better than I have in a long time. I... I'd really like to go."

That was an understatement. Silas seemed to be behind everything that made her feel good. That encouraged her and helped her. And while she loved it, it also bothered her. She didn't want to depend on just one person. She didn't want to depend on anyone. She wanted to be able to stand on her own two feet.

"But it's been a big day. And..."

He laughed a little and shook his head. "You don't need to come up with an excuse. It's not going to hurt my feelings if you just say you don't want to."

She felt like maybe it did. Maybe since the Piece Makers had put the idea of kissing Silas in her head, she had a hard time thinking of anything else. Which she wasn't complaining about, since it had definitely had the intended consequence of taking her mind off of everything else, but she had wondered if he really wanted to. Maybe he was doing it just to be nice. Even though he'd said other things.

And maybe that would complicate their relationship a little more than what she wanted to. After all, wasn't there some kind of syndrome where a person suffering from grief developed an unhealthy attachment to someone who was helping her through that grief?

Or maybe that was someone suffering a medical issue. Who fell in love with her doctor. She couldn't remember.

Regardless, as much as she couldn't get the idea of kissing Silas out of her head, until she was sure that was the direction she should go, she figured she probably should go home and spend some time alone.

"Hey, Silas. You'll love this." Brawley came into the garage, stopping short when he saw Gladys. "Oh. Am I interrupting something?"

Both Silas and Gladys laughed, exchanging glances, since that was not the first time that day they'd been asked that question, when they really hadn't been doing anything that had been interrupted.

Maybe they just looked like they were.

The thought sobered Gladys, and Silas, seeing her face, knitted his brows together like he was trying to figure out what had stolen her smile, but he didn't ask. Instead, he turned to look at his brother and said, "Nice. I'll be right out."

"Take your time," Browley said with a smirk.

"I guess maybe it's a good thing that I wasn't planning to go to your house tonight. People seem to be thinking things about us that aren't really true," Gladys said, looking around, trying to remember if she brought anything with her that she needed to take. Her mind felt a little scattered.

"Maybe we should make them true," Silas murmured, and she almost missed it.

Then her head jerked up, and her eyes narrowed. She searched his face. "Are you still trying to take my mind off things? The Piece Makers planted that idea in your head, and you can't get it out?"

She didn't want that to be true. She wanted him to want her for her, not because he was trying to help.

He shook his head but didn't say anything more. Maybe he felt like he had already said too much. When she didn't feel like he'd said enough.

"I'll see you around," she finally said when he remained silent.

"Take care," he said.

She nodded without turning, opening the door and walking out.

She had just started her car and was getting ready to pull out when she got a text from Mabel asking her to pick her up at Lark's farm, since Mabel had dropped her car off at the shop that morning for some minor repairs on her way to meet Sadie.

Sadie had driven her to Lark's on the way to the auction in Rockerton so that the two of them could get to know each other.

Gladys was grateful for the distraction. After all, she'd pretty much cut off her nose just to spite her face when she declined Silas's invitation to spend the evening with him.

She wanted to. Why hadn't she accepted?

Fear. Mostly. If she were being honest.

Her mind was a jumble as she drove down the highway. What was wrong with her? Why couldn't she make simple decisions?

What to do with her dad's business, for one. Which maybe wasn't such a simple decision, and how she felt about Silas, which should be simple but didn't feel that way.

And maybe she shouldn't be relying completely on her feelings anyway.

She knew where Lark's farm was, although she'd never been down the long drive and couldn't see the house from the road.

It was much smaller than what she had thought it would be, especially considering that Sadie had said in passing when talking about Lark that there were five or six girls living there.

As she pulled up, Lark walked out of the shed beside the barn and strode over to her car. She wore her smile like it was a permanent part of her face, her eyes crinkled, her whole demeanor radiating joy.

Gladys wasn't sure she'd ever met someone who seemed so happy without saying a word. And for no apparent reason.

Lark made it to her, with her hand held out. "I know you're Gladys, Mabel's sister, because I recognize you from seeing you around, but I don't think we've ever been introduced."

Gladys took her hand, which was rough with callouses but warm with a firm grasp, and shook it.

She couldn't remember whether Lark had been at the funeral or not. Most of it was a haze. All she remembered clearly was that Silas had been by her side.

"It's so nice to meet you, Lark. I've heard such wonderful things about you and the work you do."

If possible, Lark's smile got even bigger. "Mabel's been a blessing today. She's just eating up everything we're doing. She's going to make an awesome vet someday."

Gladys had already figured as much, but usually people were not so effusive in their praise of Mabel. Mostly because Mabel was so quiet and withdrawn.

"She's a natural with the animals. They calm down under her presence like nothing I've ever seen," Lark said, her face showing her amazement.

"We were never allowed to have animals, and Mabel wanted a pet so bad."

"I can see why. She seems to have an affinity with them that is seriously uncommon." Lark went on to talk about Mabel's ability and then surged into the fact that after Mabel had texted and asked to be picked up, they found a calf that needed some attention. So Lark was there just to let Gladys know that Mabel would be out soon.

Gladys listened, amazed at the work that Lark had done, just out of vet school, wanting to help both people and animals and finding a place on her small farm for both.

What Silas had said about talking to people who were older and wiser than her and getting advice from them ran through her mind, and while Lark wasn't older, she was farther along in her Christian walk.

Gladys had admired her almost from the second they met, just because she seemed so happy and so much different than the kinds of people she was used to. She didn't seem to worry about what Gladys may think of her, and she had no guile.

Gladys wouldn't mind getting her thoughts on some of the things that she had to think about, but it seemed like there was no opening in the conversation for them. So she just listened and made appropriate comments.

Finally, as Lark mentioned how all the girls lifted her workload on the long hours of being a vet, Gladys said, "Haven't you ever considered getting married? Then there would be two of you." She wanted to add that the girls would have a mom and dad but didn't because she didn't want to make Lark feel guilty, if there was some reason why she couldn't.

For the first time since they started talking, Lark's face fell just a little bit, although her smile did not completely slip away.

"That hasn't been a door that God has opened for me," she finally said, then her face brightened. "But I've prayed about it."

Gladys nodded, saying, "You think God brings the perfect person into your life at a certain time?"

Lark grunted a laugh. "I don't know if I believe all that about soul mates and everything. I think you can pretty much be happy with anyone as long as your values are aligned, and you're both determined to stick it out. Maybe happier with some people than others, but maybe sometimes we get too caught up in finding the perfect person and even more caught up in chasing our own happiness."

It was an interesting perspective, and Gladys found herself agreeing. Although, as she looked at Silas, she figured he was pretty much perfect, and whoever got him would be getting a really great man.

"What about you?" Lark asked, with a little laugh. She seemed to laugh a lot. "You're not married, and you're not any younger than I am."

"I'm twenty-four. And... My parents really wanted me to be married. But it just wasn't something I was interested in."

"Some of us aren't," Lark said, lifting a shoulder. "Although, I guess I always have been, but you know, sometimes you're interested in someone who's just not interested in you back." Her words sounded fatalistic, like she had long ago accepted the fact that the one she wanted didn't want her.

"Doesn't sound like you're over him," Gladys said, looking at Lark more carefully. Maybe her happy exterior hid a sad heart.

Lark seemed totally at peace. "I'm not. I guess God might have opened doors for me, and I just didn't see them, because I was stuck on the one I wanted."

"Think you'll ever get unstuck?" Gladys asked, concerned about Lark. How could she be so happy when she didn't have something she obviously wanted?

"I don't think so. Maybe I'm wrong. Maybe God just wants me to be patient with Him and wait on His timing. Or maybe He needed me to do what I'm doing now, I don't know. I just know whatever He puts in front of me, I have to do it to the best of my ability, and I can't sit around wishing I had something else or someone...that I don't."

It was the second time she'd heard that today, and it was pretty amazing to her how Lark's words echoed Silas's words almost word for word.

"That makes a lot of sense," she said sincerely.

Lark jerked her head, then shifted. "I was happy that I was going to get a couple of minutes with you because I have a question for you." Lark rubbed her hands down the front of her dusty jeans, almost as though she were nervous.

"Of course. What is it?" Gladys couldn't imagine what Lark could want, but she'd be happy to answer anything.

"You know the girls that I take in here on the farm come from homes that aren't the greatest. And I'm grateful that I'm able to do it, but sometimes I feel overwhelmed. My training is with animals. I don't have the knowledge, skills, or anything really to help them with the things they've been through."

Gladys nodded, knowing that there was wickedness in the world that was almost unimaginable. She didn't know what exactly Lark was talking about, but she didn't have any trouble imagining.

"I really feel like I need to hire someone who...maybe would be a partner? Just someone who could help me with the girls, their psychological and spiritual development, because I can keep them busy physically. And I think a lot of times that's what people need. They need to feel needed. To have a purpose. But sometimes they want to talk to me about things that happened to them, how they feel..." She threw up her hands. "I just can't always relate. My dad died when I was little, and that was hard, but I had the best mom in the world. I have the best brothers anywhere. My life has been pretty much perfect. I had an anonymous donor who donated to my schooling, so I graduated from vet school with no debt. I'm the only person I know who isn't paying off student loans."

She shook her head and shoved both hands in her back pockets.

"You don't have to answer me, and you won't hurt my feelings if it's not something you're interested in. It wouldn't be a big, prestigious job..." Lark's voice dropped a little, like she knew it was a long shot, and she figured that Gladys probably had big-city dreams.

Maybe she had at one point, but being in North Dakota had changed her. Was still changing her. She was becoming a person she liked a lot better. Less concerned about the way she looked, the image she presented, and more concerned about her heart and what she did.

Silas had instigated that change, whether he knew it or not, from back when they were just casual friends, getting together at night and drag racing together.

He had shown her what a true friend was. Still, when she looked at herself, she didn't see nearly the things she wanted to. There was always room for improvement, and that improvement probably wasn't going to happen as fast as she wanted.

"You know what...never mind," Lark said with a friendly smile, making it obvious that there truly would be no hard feelings. "I can see you trying to scrounge around and figure out a way to turn me down without hurting my feelings. It is just an idea I had. There's lots of information on the Internet, and that's what I've been trying to do, along with using my Bible, because God knows better than anyone how we should handle things, considering He made us."

"Actually, I was just thinking about how much North Dakota has changed me. And how, you're right. Not long ago, I would have turned that offer down. Because I did have some big-city dreams, but those really aren't my dreams anymore. If I went back to LA or any big city, I know I would get sucked into wanting everything to be about me." She breathed out and shook her head. "I don't mean to make it sound like everyone in the city is selfish and mean, I'm not saying that at all. I'm just saying for me, being here in North Dakota has been the best thing to ever happen to me, from a personal growth standpoint."

Lark nodded like she understood, but since she'd grown up in North Dakota, she probably didn't exactly get how different it was from the rest of the world.

"I don't know what exactly the job entails, but I want it. Count me in."

Kind of funny that God would give her the idea of whatever He put in front of her, she was to do the very best she could with, and then she struggled with the decision as to whether or not she should sell the place in North Dakota, the one that was already paid for, because there would be no jobs for counselors around here, no opportunities for her to put her degree to work, and then the Lord opened this door.

"Do you want to pray about it first?" Lark asked, like it was something everyone did before they accepted a job.

"There have been very specific signs in my life, and I'm sure this is the way I am supposed to go. But if you think I need to pray about it, I'll do that. When do you want my answer?"

"As soon as you're sure," Lark said easily.

"My answer is yes."

They laughed together as Mabel came jogging toward the car.

"I'm sorry I'm late."

"Not a problem." Gladys gave her sister a hug. "It gave Lark and I some time to talk."

Lark and she shared a smile.

She couldn't believe how much happier Mabel looked after spending the day with Lark. Like she was in an environment that nurtured her and helped her to grow rather than stifled her, which is what seemed to have been happening all her life.

She needed the connection with animals to realize her true self or maybe just to be able to utilize the gifts that God had given her.

And maybe, just maybe, one of the benefits of her parents passing was that she and Mabel had developed a stronger bond between them. Instead of having someone who lived in the same house as she did, she realized that her sister was also becoming a friend.

Chapter Twenty

Doing things God's way rather than mine. Good, clear communication and kindness.
- Cheryl Byers from Biggs, KY

Silas had work to do in his garage the evening after Gladys had been at the shop helping him watch the twins. Although when he got home, he went into the house and started making himself some supper.

Of course, he wanted Gladys there with him, but he hadn't been making things up about needing to work in his garage. Although, he supposed he wasn't above that sort of thing, if it helped him see his girl.

He figured the Piece Makers really knew what they were doing when they planted that kissing idea in his head.

He could see the Lord's hand at work as well. Just the idea that Gladys and he had been friends for so long, and had slowly grown closer, and then with her parents dying, it had lit a fire under their relationship, but they'd already built a good foundation.

Then, with the Piece Makers' prompting, it definitely had him thinking about his friend in a new way.

So yeah, he was disappointed she hadn't shown up. After changing his clothes, he'd just started working when Nolt walked into his kitchen.

"I was just wishing I had some help," he said as he heard the door slam and looked up from cooking some sausage and onion to see his brother.

"Maybe I didn't come to help. Maybe I just came to watch and make fun of you."

"That's fine too. Company is always welcome. Even if they're just here for free food." The right kind of company anyway. He supposed he could think of a few people he'd rather not spend an evening with.

"I'll keep that in mind. Maybe I'll see if the Piece Makers want to come out and spend a few late evenings watching you while you cook."

"You said you were just leaving, right?" Silas teased.

Nolt walked over and looked at the sausage in the skillet and the ingredients on the counter.

"William's One-Skillet Pasta?" he asked, although it really wasn't a question.

"Yep," Silas said, and they shared a smile, remembering their friend who had shared this recipe with them – named after his beloved only son – and had left Sweet Water to become a big-name voice actor in Hollywood. It had become an instant favorite of theirs, easy to make and also yummy. Plus, it reminded them of their friend and the success he'd had.

They chatted about the auction some, although Silas had already heard everything from his brothers when they got home. Nolt had some observations that he hadn't shared with the rest of them, and Silas listened intently. Nolt had a good head on his shoulders, and Silas really looked up to his older brother.

Their conversation had tapered off and he was adding cream and chicken broth to the sausage and onion when Nolt said, "You and Gladys looked pretty cozy when we got home. I think she's a good girl."

"For a city girl?"

"For any kind of girl." Nolt didn't smile at Silas's little bit of teasing.

Silas figured that meant Nolt wanted to be serious, which he wasn't too keen on. He didn't really want to talk about Gladys. But then he remembered his words of earlier, where he'd told her that it was always good to get a wise person's advice. Someone who was farther along in their Christian walk than he was. That definitely described Nolt.

"So what are you saying?" Silas asked, pouring noodles in and giving everything a stir before putting the lid back on and leaning a hip against the counter.

"I said she was a nice girl," Nolt replied, wringing out a rag to wipe the counter without looking up.

"But you mean she's a nice girl as in a nice girl for a friend? Or are you saying that you approve if I have a relationship with her?"

"If you want my advice, you can just ask for it," Nolt said, giving him a side glance and lifting a brow.

"Fine. Give me advice about Gladys, bro."

"You forgot the magic word?"

"Now."

Nolt coughed, then put both hands on the front of the sink and leaned over it, looking down, but Silas guessed he wasn't seeing anything. "I think you two have been friends for a long time, although I don't think a lot of people know that."

"True."

"I think she's in a hard place right now."

"She is." Silas didn't ask Nolt how he knew that.

"I think she might have been a bit of a player in Los Angeles, but I think she's starting to love North Dakota."

"I agree."

"And a certain cowboy who lives there."

"Me?" Silas wasn't expecting Nolt to come off with the L word.

"No, dummy. Your sidekick."

"I don't understand how you might know that, since you've barely seen her."

"I saw her at the funeral. I saw you two. I don't even think either one of you realized it at the time, but you bolstered each other. That's what friends do, true. And the best marriages are built on a solid friendship. Where the two of you aren't keeping score. You just give. And don't expect anything in return. Watching you two, it was obvious to me that was the kind of relationship you had. And seeing you today, it was clear there's an attraction there as well."

"So you think we can actually work?" Silas wasn't sure exactly what he meant by that question. Just... Gladys wasn't his type. He wasn't her type. They were all wrong for each other. But it felt right when they were together. But he didn't want to go by his feelings.

He wanted to do the right thing.

He lifted the lid and stirred, thinking.

"Honestly, bro. I can't see you in the city. I think it would be too much for you. I can see her here, though. But either way, yeah. I guess I came out tonight thinking that you already knew that, and I thought you two were together, even if you weren't announcing it to people."

"No. We're not. Not like that. Although, I guess we did talk about it a little bit today."

"Talk about it?"

"Well, yeah, we were talking about it, but then Marigold came and we got interrupted."

"She did okay with the babies?" Nolt asked, like that might be an issue.

"She's better with them than I am. They liked her better." He wasn't bitter about that, although he was their uncle. Still, it made his heart happy to see his nieces had such an affinity for the girl he had his eye on.

"I guess that doesn't mean anything other than she's good with kids, but I'm glad to see it. If people are good with children, it says something about their character."

"Yeah. I guess I thought that as well." He wouldn't use that to judge anyone, but he had enjoyed seeing her with them. Seeing that she enjoyed them, that she wasn't afraid to hold them or change diapers, and that she didn't get flustered when they cried. He supposed that just showed him she was okay being a servant and didn't need to have everyone in her vicinity orbiting around her. That was all.

The noodles were cooked, so he added the cheese and stirred. Nolt set two plates and silverware on the table and they ate together, still talking but leaving the subject of Gladys to rest. Which Silas appreciated. He wanted Nolt's wisdom, but he didn't want to have to make a decision about anything tonight. He wanted to think. He wanted to be sure that he wasn't running ahead of Gladys and what she wanted, too.

They finished eating and cleaned up and Nolt left shortly after. Silas wasn't the slightest bit tired, so he headed out to the garage, looking around and trying to decide what type of job he wanted to get into. Something mindless, but something that would get his hands dirty. He wanted to be elbow deep in something and not thinking about Gladys and whether or not she might like him too, and especially not about kissing her.

Two hours later, he had grease up to the elbows on both arms and was digging deep into the engine when the door opened and the person he was trying not to think about walked in.

He looked up and didn't have the presence of mind not to do a double take. He also couldn't keep from smiling.

But he straightened slowly, unsure of what she wanted, because her look was so serious.

"Hey," she said softly.

"Hey. Good to see you."

Her eyes crinkled just a bit at that, although she didn't respond, just said, "Do you have a few minutes to talk to me?"

His stomach did a slow dive, and his heart dropped after it. "Let me wash my hands."

She nodded, coming in, closing the door, and walking over.

Normally when he was around Gladys, the silences never felt awkward, and he never scrambled for something to fill them. But tonight, for some reason he was racking his brain for something to say to throw out into the emptiness that seemed to expand between them. For the first time since he could remember, he felt self-conscious in front of her, like she was judging him for the dirt on his hands.

Or watching that he made sure to get it all off.

He wasn't sure, it just felt...uncomfortable. Like his stomach after eating at a buffet.

He wasn't successful in thinking of anything to talk about, so he washed and dried his hands in silence before he turned around and just flat-out asked, "What did you need?"

She closed the three feet between them with confident strides, and he almost felt like he was being stalked, like prey.

There was no place for him to back up, so as casually as he could, he leaned back against the sink, intending to put his arms over his chest, but she didn't give him that opportunity. She didn't stop until their torsos were pressed together and her arms were around his neck, their faces mere inches apart.

His breath caught in his throat, and he felt like he was choking on his heart which was beating so hard he figured she could probably hear it.

His palms were sweating, but rather than wiping them down the front of his jeans like he wanted to, he brought them up to land softly on either side of her hips.

Not pulling, just resting there.

"You're scaring me a little, Gladys," he finally said, and his voice wasn't quite normal.

But that was the truth. Was this goodbye?

Their relationship had never been like this before. He hadn't talked much, a lot of the time they were together, but she never stalked him. Never pushed him. And had never been this physical.

He supposed it could be the other way around, and she was trying to say she wanted more with him, but Gladys was never the one that had trouble with words.

That was him.

"Good."

He looked for the smile on her face, something to let him know that she was joking, that this was some little thing she was doing, and they would soon go back to normal, but he saw nothing but dead seriousness.

"If you're leaving North Dakota, just say so."

"I'm not."

It took a little bit for her words to sink in.

"You're not?"

She shook her head, her body moving a little bit, and he almost closed his eyes over the sweet friction. "No. Lark asked me to take a counseling job with her. When she said it, what you had said rang so clear in my mind, because she had just said something almost exactly the same."

"What was that?" He said a lot of things. Hopefully it wasn't one of the things he'd said that made her decide to leave. But she said she was staying.

"It was when you said that whatever God puts in front of you, you just put your hand to it and do it to the best of your ability. You don't shrug your shoulders and walk away from it, or find excuses to not do it, or look around for something better."

He remembered that. "When the twins were there."

"Yeah."

He hadn't realized she'd been paying attention. Sometimes he felt like he talked and it just went out to empty air. It was nice to talk to someone who actually remembered the words he said. Not just remembered them, but acted on them.

It made him feel like she cared.

He hoped she got the same feeling from him. Did he pay attention to what she said? He thought he did.

"So I start next Monday."

"And you're staying?"

"I'm staying."

"And your parents' business?"

"The accountant is going ahead, and the sales are going through, and I've already talked to their lawyer. Everything that Dad was putting in motion will stay in motion."

He nodded, still a little baffled because she wasn't quite acting the way she normally did. Her arms around his neck and her fingers lightly playing with the hair on the back of it. It made him shiver and want to pull her closer.

But he still felt excited, barely able to contain the way his whole body wanted to jump up and down like a two-year-old offered ice cream.

"That's good news."

"It is. But it's not the reason I'm here tonight."

Her fingers brushed over the back of his neck again, and her eyes glowed as she saw him unable to contain his shiver.

"That was a good shiver." There was no doubt in her voice.

"The best."

Her fingers ran over the back of his neck again, which did not elicit a shiver this time but felt just as good. He fought to keep his eyes open.

She smiled the way he imagined a tiger would smile right before it pounced.

"So you gonna tell me why you're here?" he asked, talking before he couldn't. His throat was about to betray him, and his mouth was already so dry he couldn't swallow.

"For your kissing lesson," she said, like it was the most obvious thing in the world.

He couldn't keep from giving her a slow smile that curled his lips up. "Finally."

He had to tease her a little. Kissing Gladys had been pretty much the only thing he thought of all day. Even though he hadn't seen her since she left, she was always in his head. Funny how an idea could get planted and grow and take over his every waking thought.

"But I just want to be clear about something," she said, her gaze looking straight into his eyes.

She could be clear about anything, just as long as she quit talking and started kissing within a reasonable amount of time. Like, before he ran out of air, since he felt like his lungs had quit working.

"What's that?" he asked, pushing the words out.

"You don't need lessons."

Disappointment almost made him double over. "What do you mean?" His hands tightened on her hips, and her eyes flickered.

"I mean that I don't need to tell you to pay attention to me, and I don't need to tell you to be gentle, and I don't need to explain to you what you need to do in order to make me feel loved and cherished and like I am the most important thing in the world to you. And I don't care if you slobber all over me, or if your technique isn't the best in the world, or if you don't kiss the way the rest of the world thinks you should."

"You don't?" He wasn't following her. The quilting ladies had told him that all of those things were important.

"I don't. And I'm not going to."

He gritted his teeth. He'd suspected she was breaking up with him. It was an odd way to do it, but that's what it seemed like. Not that they were even together. How could she break up with him if they'd never officially been together?

Wait.

"You said you were here to give me lessons."

"Let me clarify. I'm here to tell you that you don't need lessons."

"So...I don't get it."

She kept his mind going in circles. How was he supposed to follow the reasoning that she was here to give him kissing lessons when she then said he didn't need lessons, and now she was just standing there looking at him, and all he wanted to do was kiss her, but she didn't want that.

He shook his head a little, trying to clear it.

"I'm saying, Silas, I don't care how you kiss. Because it doesn't matter. Because you already make me feel like the most beautiful woman in the world, like nothing matters to you except me, when you look at me the way you're looking at me right now. I just want to be closer to you, whatever that looks like."

He thought she was saying... "You want to be closer?"

She grinned a little, as though finding amusement in the fact that was the one thing he'd latched onto out of all the things she'd said.

"Yes."

"Me too."

She smiled and lifted one brow like she was waiting. And maybe she was.

Silas lifted his hands from her hips, moving them around to the small of her back, and he lowered his head, touching her lips with his, carefully. Remembering what the ladies and Gladys herself had said about being gentle.

He wasn't sure exactly what that meant, but he cradled the back of her head like it was the most precious thing in the world to him, and maybe Gladys was. He couldn't think of anything else that meant more.

And maybe gentleness just equaled consideration. Which was the equivalent of showing her how important she was to him.

Then, his lips slid across hers again, and she sighed, and he forgot about thinking about consideration and gentleness and kissing and whether he was any good at it or not, and just focused on her lips moving under his and her body moving under his hand and her hair sliding through his fingers and the heat that filled his chest, his racing heart, his lungs that didn't seem to work, that couldn't get enough air, while his whole being agreed with Gladys. They weren't close enough.

He wasn't sure which one of them pulled away first, but it was just a little movement, maybe him because he needed to breathe. But he didn't want to break the physical connection he had with her, so he pulled back enough that he could suck in air but still brush his lips over hers.

"Sorry if I slobbered," he said, wishing he had the romantic words that women loved.

Although, come to think of it, she had never said anything about romantic words when she talked about teaching him to kiss.

"You never apologized for the things you need to apologize for." Her voice was husky and a little breathless.

"I'm supposed to be apologizing about something else?" He kissed the corner of her mouth, her chin, and ran his thumb over the line of her jaw, holding her head still so he could press his lips against hers once more.

"For making my knees weak, and turning my brain to mush, and making me feel like I can't breathe, can't think, can't imagine anything except kissing you again."

"You're right. I'm not apologizing for any of that."

Her words were the exact right ones to make him feel like maybe her declaration that he didn't need kissing lessons had been true and accurate. Maybe she would be happy with whatever he had.

"Aren't you gonna tell me how I can improve?"

Maybe that was a little of his insecurity coming out. She had probably been kissed a lot more than he had. He hadn't really been thinking about technique. Although he meant to. He had meant to kiss her with all the ability and skill he had, which wasn't saying much, but he'd use everything he had for her. But he hadn't even been thinking about it, just wanted to be closer. Wanted to have that connection, that good feeling, that right feeling that the girl he was holding was the one he was meant to hold for the rest of his life.

"I would, but there's nothing to say." She lifted her shoulders a little and smiled up at him. "In fact, I think you should be the one giving me pointers. I want your knees to be weak, and your brain to be mush, and your lungs to forget how to work, leaving you breathless."

"You've already done that and a whole lot more."

She tilted her head. "Are you sure?"

He nodded. "Positive."

"I don't think so."

This was an argument he could get into, but before he could say anything else, she said, "I'm pretty sure I need a lot more practice. Do you know anybody who would be willing to help me?"

He laughed, laughed because she knew she didn't have to do anything special or pretend to need practice in order to get him to want to kiss her again, but he liked that she did. That she was showing him that she wanted more too.

"Actually, now that I think about it, maybe there was that one part where you need a little work."

"Which part was that?" she asked, and maybe she batted her eyes a little.

"I'm not sure. I think we need to start from the beginning, do it all again, and I'll let you know when we get to the part where my knees are weak but not weak enough."

"You do that."

They smiled at each other before his head lowered again, and they kissed for a very long time.

Chapter Twenty-One

A healthy church (Jesus) life!
- Stephanie Frost from Fremont, NE

They had the kissing part down anyway.

Gladys was still smiling several days later as she checked her reflection in the hall mirror before she answered the door. Silas had slid from friend to...more so naturally. And kissing Silas had become her favorite pastime.

She couldn't believe that Silas had rung the doorbell, but she'd heard it from upstairs where she was getting ready and hurried down to meet him.

She opened the door, a big smile on her face that froze, then slowly fell off as her brain processed the fact that it was not Silas standing at the door.

"Obviously...you were expecting someone else," the man said, and his voice sounded familiar, although she couldn't place him.

"You must be one of my dad's friends."

"James. We spoke on the phone not long ago."

"I remember you." She took his proffered hand and shook it, liking the way he looked in her eyes and that his grip was firm but not too tight, and he didn't hold onto her hand but let it go immediately.

"I know we agreed that I wasn't coming anymore, but..." He grinned sheepishly. "I was going to say how I was in the area and thought I'd stop by anyway, but there really isn't anything in the area to be here for, so...I made a special trip." He shrugged his shoulders, and his grin was boyish and endearing.

Gladys liked him despite herself, the way she might like a younger brother.

"Why don't you come on in," she said, opening the door wider and standing back.

"Are you sure? You look like you were expecting someone else."

"I am. But you're welcome too. You've come a long way."

"I was hoping maybe...Mabel was here." He said the last part low, almost like he was afraid she would be in the house to hear him or that it might upset Gladys to hear him say that.

When they talked on the phone, he had been clear about his interest in Mabel.

"She's been helping a veterinarian who lives down the road from us a ways. They're out on a call, and she's not going to be in until late. In fact, she said she might not be back at all, but we'll see her tomorrow night."

His face fell, and he seemed dejected.

"I'm sorry," she said.

Maybe if he'd have called first, she could have asked Mabel to come home, but she hated to have her miss even a second of all the things that she'd missed all of her life.

"No. You mentioned how she feels about animals, and I'm sure she's enjoying her time with the vet. I wouldn't want to take her from that."

James impressed her even more with his words, and she found herself wishing that Mabel truly was there. But then she realized that was not feasible.

"She still has four years left of vet school. Well, two years of school, and then she needs to intern for two years. She really needs to focus on her studies."

"I get it. I got my master's degree, so I know that postgraduate studies are not easy, but I just really wanted to see her."

"It might be best if you wait until she's done."

"I'd gladly wait if I knew she was waiting too. But she might have found someone else by then."

Gladys couldn't believe that this man would be so interested in Mabel that he'd wait for four years, because in her experience, most men lost interest quickly when their interest wasn't returned.

"I suppose you could ask her if she's interested and that she'd give you a chance when she's ready." Gladys was just grasping at straws, something to appease this man whom she liked more and more the more time she spent with him.

"I guess. But that hardly seems fair, since I know her better than she knows me."

"How do you know her?"

"She used to go with your dad on business trips to San Antonio. That's where I was at the time, and I remember seeing her with him. She was still in high school, and of course I couldn't be interested because of her age, but she intrigued me. I've followed her on social media ever since."

Gladys's eyebrows shot way out. "I know Mabel is on social media, but I can't believe she posts anything."

"Not much. Although, since she started working with Dr. Lark, she's posted more."

Gladys could believe that. Mabel had really come out of her shell, if that's what one could call it. She just seemed to come alive since she started working for Dr. Lark.

"I could give you Dr. Lark's phone number, and you could call her."

A knock at the door interrupted her, and it opened. That's what she expected from Silas, and she smiled, moving toward him and almost completely forgetting about James who backed out of the way.

"Hey there," she said, knowing she probably looked like a grinning fool but loving that he was here. Even though she'd seen him earlier that day when she stopped in at the garage to eat lunch with him.

"Hey, yourself," he said, returning her grin, his eyes running over the hair that she'd fixed carefully and the jeans and tunic shirt she'd picked out, going for casual chic. She wasn't sure if she accomplished the look or not, but she did get the look from Silas that she'd been aiming for, so it didn't really matter what she actually looked like.

"I'm Silas," Silas said, wrapping one arm around Gladys and reaching over and holding his hand out to James.

"James." James clasped his hand and said, "I was here asking about Mabel. Gladys was just about to give me Dr. Lark's number so I might be able to have a few words with her."

Silas jerked his head, then he said, "She has a lot of school in front of her."

James nodded, a little self-consciously. "That's what Gladys was just saying. I know. And I'll wait. I just...don't want her to get caught away by someone else in the meantime."

"Sometimes things are meant to happen. And sometimes they're not." Silas wasn't smiling, and his words came out more like a warning.

Gladys appreciated the fact that he wasn't even related to Mabel, but he was protecting her, just like he would his own sister, because of Gladys.

She squeezed his waist and tucked in closer to him, wanting him to know how she appreciated him and what he was doing.

His hand moved from her shoulder down her arm and back up, almost as though he were acknowledging her unspoken words with unspoken words of his own.

"I'm not pushing for anything, if that's what you're concerned about. I just... She's just someone I can't get out of my head, and it's not like I'm going to accidentally run into her somewhere, so if I want to talk to her, I'm going to have to seek her out."

"I see." Silas said, and his tone was noncommittal, but then he said, "I suppose I appreciate you wanting to meet her face-to-face rather than just sending a text or email or message, which is safer, easier, and less risky for you."

"That's what I thought. It would mean more if I showed up in person."

Silas nodded, although his expression was still stern.

Gladys pulled her phone out of her pocket, pulling up Lark in her contacts. "Are you ready for her number?"

James pulled his phone out of his pocket, swiping and clicking and then nodding.

She rattled it off, and he took it easily.

"I'll leave you two. Have a nice evening." James moved toward the door, and Silas and Gladys moved out of his way.

"Maybe we'll be seeing you around eventually," Silas said, and Gladys got the feeling that he felt the same way she did—impressed with James and his demeanor and the way he was handling things with Mabel.

They shook hands before James walked out and the door closed behind him.

"I liked that guy," Silas said, sounding surprised.

"That's funny. Because the longer I talked to him, the more I liked him too."

"But Mabel has a lot of school ahead of her. She doesn't need to be distracted by a man."

"She's never been the slightest bit interested in men. Of course, she didn't exactly have boys buzzing around her, as quiet and withdrawn as she was."

"Did your parents ever worry about her?"

"Maybe that's why Dad took her on so many trips with him. She just... She never gave them any trouble. She always got good grades. She just always seemed happier by herself."

Gladys supposed if her parents had been more alert, Mabel might have been diagnosed with some type of autism or at least something on that spectrum. But it didn't really matter. She was turning into a functioning member of society, and maybe she just needed her growing-up years to come into herself.

Regardless, it was too late to ask those questions now, and her parents weren't exactly around to ask why nothing was done.

Mabel seemed to be happy and making a life for herself. And she had a suitor. A good man in James.

"I suppose we'll never hear how that conversation went," Silas said thoughtfully as they walked to the kitchen, holding hands.

"I can ask Mabel tomorrow. You know, I was thinking the other day that was something good that's come out of my parents' accident. Mabel and I have gotten closer."

"I'm happy for you two."

He tugged on her hand, and she looked up, wondering what he wanted, but she recognized the wolfish gleam in his eye.

"I missed my lesson today."

"You're saying you think you need more lessons?"

"If that's what you want to call it."

"You have a better name?"

Instead of answering her, his face lost its smile and he got serious. "After you left the garage the other night, I realized that maybe I got the cart ahead of the horse a little bit."

"Meaning?"

"I love you. I knew it that night, I knew that's why I couldn't stop thinking about you, couldn't stop thinking about kissing you, but more than that, thinking about things I could do to make you smile. Things you might enjoy. And anything I did, I thought of how much better it would be if you were with me." He shrugged. "Then we started kissing, and I forgot to tell you that I love you."

"I love you too. And I love everything you just said."

"So go ahead. Give me the pretty words too."

"How about we just kiss instead?"

He grinned. "That's fine too."

He leaned his head down, but James's arrival had reminded her of something she couldn't believe she'd forgotten.

With their noses almost touching, she said, "Marry me."

She laughed at the comical look on his face. He stopped, started to jerk back, then obviously corrected himself, although his hands were still squeezing her way too tight, and she wiggled a little to let him know he needed to loosen his grip.

"Sorry. You just..."

"I surprised you. Shocked. You're flabbergasted. Pretty much gobsmacked."

"Yeah. All that. Times ten."

"I think that's a no."

"No. That's a give me a minute to recover. That's a I wasn't expecting to tell her I love her and get her to propose marriage to me."

"I was just thinking about my inheritance."

He straightened, all tenderness and humor leaving his face. "I guess I'd forgotten it, but it doesn't really mean anything to me. We'll just let it go. There's no point in rushing things just because we'll get a bunch of money if we do. That's not the way I want to do things."

She really appreciated those words. Appreciated the fact that the money didn't mean anything to him. Not that she was concerned that it had, she just loved knowing, loved seeing the action of him wanting her and not caring about her money. Although, the fact that he hadn't even made a move for her until her parents were gone and she admitted that she was destitute had already convinced her that any interest he had had been purely for her.

"It's not that I don't want to," he said, maybe misinterpreting her silence as hurt. "Because I do. But I'm not sure you're ready, and while I know I am, I don't want you to do anything that you'll regret or that you feel pushed into."

"I don't feel pushed. It's what I want, or I wouldn't have said anything. The money is secondary, so don't go thinking that I'm just marrying you so I can get my inheritance."

"That's what I thought. I figured I was just the route to your inheritance." He grinned, letting her know that his words were totally sarcastic, and she laughed.

"I don't think either one of us could pretend like that."

"I don't think so either. At least, I hope not."

"Think about it, would you?"

"Think about marrying you? That's an easy yes."

"Goodness, it took you long enough to say so."

"Well, you mentioned money in the same breath as marrying me, and it made me feel like that's all I was to you, just a paycheck."

"That's my line."

"You're the one who started the whole marriage business."

She loved this side of Silas. His teasing side, which she hadn't seen much, but she hoped to see more of.

"So what do you think?" she asked. "I don't want to push you either, but you said you're ready. And I am too. And I don't see any reason to postpone it when we could be millionaires if we don't."

"I guess... That much money makes me nervous. Because, when you start getting a lot of things, a lot of money, it can change you. I don't want money to change us. To become more important to us than what we are to each other."

She thought that was wise, but she still hated the idea of losing the money, although it was good to her to know that it wasn't some kind of male pride thing to him, where he didn't want to take the money because it was hers and he didn't provide it. Although she could respect that, because she understood that men did have a certain amount of pride. It was part of what made them male.

"We have a few months. I don't turn twenty-five until this fall. Can we think about it?"

"Let's do that. That is, not make a decision either way, but give ourselves another month or two to think about it, and then it doesn't take that long to get married, so we can do it," he promised. "Unless you want a big wedding? I understand those take a lot of time to plan."

"No. I don't. I found that the simpler I live, the happier I am." And it was true. Getting rid of the property in LA, letting her dad's business go, having everything off her shoulders other than the house she lived in and the job in front of her made things easy.

"I love that. I think that's probably true too. We kind of get caught up in stuff and having more and doing more and working harder to get even more, and I think we forget that that's not really what life's about."

"No. But when God puts something in front of you, you put your hand to it, and you do it with all your might. Sometimes, you might make money while you're doing it."

"I definitely agree. God promises that He'll not just bless our work, but when we give to other people, He says that men will give to us. Not Him, men."

"So if we get married and inherit the money, we'll have a lot of money to give away."

"You can definitely get me on board with that. I can think of a lot of places it could be used, including with Lark. She could use a bigger house."

"You can say that again. There are five girls there, and with Lark, that's six, and when Mabel stays over, it's seven. There are only two bedrooms."

They started to get food out and didn't say anything for a bit. Maybe he was thinking about the things they could do with the money; she knew she was. Not for themselves, although, she supposed she would want to keep some back, just in case they had children and they needed a college fund.

Maybe some investments.

And for some reason, her mind drifted off to a subject she hadn't thought about for a while.

"You know we're going to have to pay the Piece Makers a visit."

"We do?" He stopped with a bag of flour in his hand, turning and looking at her in confusion.

"Sure. It would only be right to let them know that their scheme worked." She grinned, and he got it right away.

"You mean you want to go and let them know that we were on to them the whole time, and we decided to get together anyway."

"I suppose we could let them know that too, if you really feel the need to."

"Or we could just let them go on in ignorance, thinking that we were totally duped and that they're cunning and crafty and—"

"And they'll have someone else in their sights. Some other poor, unsuspecting person who is going to be subjected to their schemes."

"Wait. Hold up. That sounded a little harsh. I mean, I know you were subjected to their schemes, but come on, look what you ended up with." Silas lifted both arms away from his sides in a *look at me* gesture.

"I don't want them to take credit for that," Gladys said, putting the chicken on the counter and walking over and sliding her arms around his waist. "I want everyone to know I chose this myself."

"This?"

"You. And the kissing. I definitely choose the kissing."

Epilogue

Charlene looked up from hand-stitching pieces of fabric together for their latest quilt as the church basement door opened.

Her hands stilled as two people she didn't expect to see walked in.

Silas and Gladys.

They were holding hands. Big smiles on their faces.

Charlene smiled to herself but rose from her chair and tried to pretend she wasn't doing a victory dance on the inside. Their scheme had worked.

She noted to herself that kissing lessons were very effective in getting couples together.

"Hello!" she said as she walked toward the couple, Vicki on her right and Teresa and Kathy following.

"Good morning, ladies," Silas said, his voice sounding happier than Charlene could ever remember. Finding the right woman did that for a man.

And Gladys practically glowed. A man like Silas had that effect on the girl he cherished. And no doubt, Silas would cherish Gladys. That's just the kind of man he was. Hopefully Gladys knew what a blessed woman she was.

Charlene almost lost the thread of the conversation around her as her mind drifted to her own beloved Charley. Confident, maybe arrogant, even, with keen intelligence and a sharp wit. And he cherished her. She was blessed.

"And we just wanted to thank you for your part in it." Silas finished speaking as Charlene's focus came back to the conversation.

"The kissing lessons are what did it?" Teresa asked, always wanting to make sure. She hadn't been onboard with the kissing lessons, anyway.

"Yep. Or maybe it was just the thought of kissing. Once you get that thought in your head..." Silas's voice drifted off and he looked down at Gladys, snuggled up tight next to him.

"It's a good thought," Gladys murmured, looking up into his eyes.

The sight was sweet and tender and it made Charlene's heart sigh. Young love, right at the beginning when things were new and kisses were sweet and there was no heartache or pain between them. If they did it right, it could stay that way.

Oh, of course, infatuation faded and the rose colored glasses fell off and the newness faded, but if they stayed respectful and considerate of each other, kept the needs and wants of the other as more important than their own, didn't give more attention or effort to anyone or anything else, made time for each other and didn't forget to say the words the other needed to hear, there didn't need to be hurt and heartache.

But that was a long list and hard to do.

Especially without the experience of life behind them, reminding them to appreciate what they had, since not everyone got a beautiful, life-time love.

Still, Charlene knew Silas and Gladys would be together forever, even if they ended up going through some self-inflicted pain and tears. Those could strengthen a marriage if handled well. Trials always could.

They left shortly after and the door had barely shut before the ladies in the basement formed a circle, smiling and congratulating themselves.

Charlene allowed herself one more moment of triumph before she said, "We need to move on to the next one."

"Who's next?" Vicki asked eagerly.

It was always easier to get the ladies onboard when they were fresh off a roaring success. It was big of Silas and Gladys to come in and thank them personally.

Charlene pretended to think, although she already knew who she wanted.

"I think Nolt Powers could use us."

"Nolt Powers?" Teresa asked. "But he's pining over some girl he knew in high school, and, last I heard, that girl was married."

"She is. She's not right for Nolt, anyway. He's infatuated with an ideal that he created back when he knew her. She's not what he thinks she is."

"So...we're going to change her?" Kathy asked, somewhat timidly. Obviously she didn't see how they could accomplish something so crazy.

"I'm not good with that. I don't believe in divorce. Even if she deserves someone better than she's married to, marriage is sacred, and I'm not breaking a bond that God put together." Teresa was firm in her statement, giving each word a little punch with a nod of her head.

"Relax, ladies. You're thinking about this all wrong. It's Nolt we're going to change."

"Nolt?" Kathy gasped. "But...he's set in his ways. Not in a bad way, but when a man like that falls in love, it's forever. We're not going to change him."

"I don't think he was in love. And that's gibberish anyway. Falling in love is a very modern idea."

"What about Romeo and Juliet? They fell in love."

"Fictional characters."

"Shakespeare wrote it."

"Ladies, we can argue about this some other time." Charlene put a hand up. They needed to focus. "You're right. Nolt is our most difficult attempt yet. We need focus and determination."

"And creativity. Kissing lessons was absolutely genius." Vicki rubbed her hands together in relish.

"Possibly. Although Nolt is used to taking care of his younger brothers. It will be hard to trick him and even harder to get him to do anything he doesn't want to do. We need to have our eyes open for opportunity and come prepared to fight to win."

"I feel like I'm on a football team," Kathy said, her lower lip sticking out slightly.

"There's nothing wrong with that. This is a pre-game pep talk." Charlene clapped her hands together. "Although there will be no butt patting on my watch."

"Good to know." Teresa shivered. She wasn't a touchy-feely lady. Charlene almost got side-tracked thinking of Teresa and her love life. Maybe Charlene could help...No. She needed to focus on Nolt. He was going to be a challenge for sure.

But he was a good man – a very good man – and he deserved a good woman. Not to mention, he would treat that woman the way God commanded a man to treat his wife, which, in Charlene's opinion, was the most important characteristic of a man – his determination to love his wife more than he loved himself.

Charlene felt renewed determination. They could do this.

"Ladies, listen closely. Here's what we're going to do." She leaned forward and the other ladies followed suit as she spelled out exactly how they were going to get the unemotional and commanding Nolt Powers to fall in love. Her plan was brilliant, even if she had to say so herself.

∽

Join Jessie's list and be the first to know about new releases and sales on her books!

Read Cowboy Dreaming Alone, the next book in the Coming Home to North Dakota series. Nolt Powers gets his girl! He cares for Shasta, then an accident almost takes his life. Shasta returns the favor. Keep reading for a sneak peek now.

Sneak Peek of Cowboy Dreaming Alone

Overlooking small things.
- Paula Hurdle from Mississippi

"That's gorgeous! Even better than I had pictured!" Sadie exclaimed as she looked at the mailbox that Shasta Bingley had just handed her.

Shasta smiled, although she tried not to show her relief. Her last client had been a huge job, a wall mural that had taken her a month, and he still hadn't paid her.

She had been hoping that Sadie would like her work on the decorative mailbox, and she'd been hoping even harder that Sadie would pay her.

Today.

"I'm so glad you like it." Truly, that was the best part of her job, seeing the expressions on her clients' faces when they saw her work.

But expressions didn't pay the bills. She tried not to hold her breath as Sadie exclaimed over the intricate details of the flowers and the bird's nest and even the shiny blue robin eggs that were nestled in it.

"This mailbox is a work of art. I feel like I should mount this in my living room and not have it sitting out on my driveway." Sadie ran a gentle finger over an intricately painted daisy. "It's just breathtaking."

Sadie's appreciation was almost enough to make Shasta forget about the overdue rent, her empty cupboards, and her even more empty stomach.

She'd grown up in Nebraska and had met Sadie in college where they'd been roommates all four years. Sadie had talked so well about Sweet Water, North Dakota, that Shasta had vowed to move there as soon as she was able.

The thing she hadn't thought of, and now felt stupid about, was that in a small town, there were very few clients who would be interested in, or could afford, the kind of work she did.

Sadie loved her work, but Shasta had a hunch that Sadie had ordered the mailbox more out of pity than because she really wanted it.

Still, she wasn't too proud to take pity work right now. She needed everything she could get, and she needed to be paid for it, too.

"And these hummingbirds. They're so lifelike! You have definitely gotten better than you were even in college, and you amazed me then."

Shasta had painted everything she could get her hands on in college. She'd even gotten in trouble for painting on the walls of her dorm. But rather than fining her, the college had just made her stay and help the contractors repaint all the walls in the dorms during summer break.

It hadn't been too bad, because after she put in her required hours, the contractor had hired her, and she had a job the rest of the summer.

It wasn't the kind of painting she loved, but it was a job, first of all, and second, every day she got to make big, white canvases and paint them in her mind with all kinds of beautiful things.

"Don't you think so, Nolt?" Sadie said, looking behind Shasta.

Shasta had been lost in her head and hadn't been paying attention, so it surprised her when a man walked up beside her, leaning over, indulgence on his face until he actually started looking at the work, and his expression soon turned to sharp interest.

Nolt, Sadie's brother.

While she'd only seen him once, he had the same tall, broad-shouldered, confident look that she had admired from afar while in college. From afar because Nolt was twelve years older than his sister, Sadie. Twelve years older than herself, and in college, twelve years was a lifetime.

She'd never told Sadie that she'd secretly crushed on her oldest brother, partly because the idea was so preposterous, and also partly because Sadie had already confided in her that Nolt had fallen in love in high school, but his crush had chosen someone else, and he'd never gotten over it.

Sadie had said he was one of those who fall in love one time and only once in a lifetime kind of guys.

Regardless, she was definitely not in a position to be in a relationship anyway. She'd struggled since college to make a living with her art, usually having to have side jobs like waitressing that had nothing to do with how she truly wanted to make her living.

Here in Sweet Water, unless she worked on a ranch, or in a trucking company, or for the feed mill, there wasn't much else since the diner wasn't hiring.

"It's good," Nolt finally said, straightening up and glancing at her with an expression that Shasta could only term disinterest.

She didn't look at him long, though, because she had another coughing fit. She turned her head and put her arm over her mouth, coughing into her elbow.

The coughing had gotten worse since it started a couple of days ago, and she felt like she was going to cough up a lung.

If she were taking stock of her symptoms, she would say she felt feverish, but she couldn't afford to not work, and she couldn't afford to be sick, so she decided it was just a little warm in the office. At least that's what she told herself.

"That cough sounds serious," Sadie said with concern.

Shasta coughed for a couple more seconds before she cleared her throat and swallowed. "It's nothing."

She thought she heard Nolt snort but couldn't say for sure.

Regardless, Sadie lifted her brows and said, "You probably ought to get it checked out."

"I will," Shasta said, cringing a little inside, because the words were most likely not true. She couldn't afford to eat, let alone go to the doctor. She'd do it if she could, so maybe she got bonus points for it being true if it were possible.

Still, the lie didn't sit well, and she stared at the floor, knowing she should probably take her leave but staying for just a few more seconds, because she was really hoping Sadie would remember to pay her.

"Something like that must cost a fortune," Nolt said, causing Shasta to smile. He'd said it was good, like it was an elementary school art project.

Maybe he liked it after all.

"Oh! You almost let me forget to pay you." Sadie pulled out a drawer in her desk and took her purse out, pulling out her wallet and a checkbook.

Sadie almost groaned. It was Friday evening, and the banks were closed. Monday was the Fourth of July, and she wouldn't be able to cash that check until Tuesday.

At least she'd had the twenty dollars required to open an account in town. So she had a bank; she just couldn't use it until Tuesday.

Still, she smiled gratefully and thanked Sadie as she ripped the check out of the book and handed it over.

SNEAK PEEK OF COWBOY DREAMING ALONE

"This mailbox might be really good advertisement for you, as much as it kills me to think of it sitting outside along the road. People will see it, and it will definitely be a conversation starter." Sadie beamed, excited. "I'm sure it will earn you a lot of work and requests for not just mailboxes but a ton of different things. You can paint anything."

Shasta gave Sadie a grateful smile, even though she had to disagree. "You've always believed in me. Thank you." So many people hadn't. And a lot of people had been right, telling her that she would never make a living from her art and she should choose a major in college that would actually pay the bills and do art on the side.

It was reasonable advice, and she probably should have taken it, but she wanted to study art, and she went all in. Determined that if she put everything she had into it, it would have to work out.

Nope. That was wrong. Even if she put her heart and soul and everything she had, literally, into her art, it didn't mean it was going to work out.

It didn't even mean that she was going to eat.

"It's Friday evening," Nolt said quietly from beside her. She'd almost forgotten he was even there.

Shasta wasn't sure what to say. If Sadie didn't pay her cash, she wouldn't be eating until Tuesday. But not only did she hate to admit her desperate straits, she hated even worse admitting them in front of Nolt. Also, she didn't want to put anyone out. The mailbox had only been a couple hundred dollars, but who carried that kind of cash around?

Before she could figure out what she was going to say, which would most likely have been a polite refusal, Nolt was pulling his wallet out of his back pocket.

"How much was it?" he asked, and when Shasta looked up, he wasn't looking at her but at his sister.

Sadie rattled off the amount, and Nolt pulled the bills from his wallet.

He held his wallet in such a way that Shasta couldn't see what all was in it, even if she had been seriously looking, which she wasn't. She was just peeking out of the corner of her eye. But it wasn't like he was flashing his money or anything. That would have been ostentatious and a real turnoff. It wasn't like that at all. And she couldn't help feeling grateful for his consideration.

"I'm sorry, I never even thought."

"It's okay. Normally I would be protesting rather strongly right now," Shasta said as she pulled the check out of her pocket and handed it to Sadie who ripped it up. "But I just did a month-long project for a man in Nebraska where I lived, it was a huge wall mural, and he hasn't paid me for it."

"And moving is expensive." Nolt made that comment like it was the most natural thing in the world, although Shasta knew for a fact that the man had never lived anywhere but Sweet Water, North Dakota.

"It is. And I needed first and last months' rent on my place here in town, and it just wiped me out." Plus getting there, a couple nights of lodging as she looked for an apartment, and little odds and ends that cropped up. Including a flat tire along the interstate.

She literally had nothing, other than a place to lay her head. Actually, her apartment didn't even boast a bed or couch. Although she did have a kitchen chair that had been left there by the last occupant.

Nolt held out the cash, and she took it, murmuring a thank you, which triggered another coughing spell.

"You need Sadie to take you to the critical care center in Rockerton?" Nolt asked when she was finally done.

She shook her head, not wanting to say anything and trigger more. She was already embarrassed enough. Coughing, needing cash, and now obviously they assumed that she wasn't adult enough to take herself to the doctor if she needed to.

Which was true, but still.

"Are you sure?" Sadie asked, concern etched on her brow.

"Yes."

The room spun. Shasta tried to concentrate to keep from swaying and losing her balance. That last coughing fit had been the worst, and she wanted to go to her apartment and lie down. On the floor, but at least she had a towel she could use as a pillow.

At any rate, she needed to get out of here before she fell. She didn't want to bother these people anymore. They had already been more kind than she deserved.

Once she'd lain down for a bit, maybe she'd be able to get up and get some groceries. Now that she could afford it.

And some cough medicine.

Giving Sadie a hug and waving at Nolt who nodded his head, she hurried out as fast as she could, determined to get some rest before she worried about how she was going to earn money.

Lord. Please send work.

Sign up for Jessie's newsletter! Get a free book, access to exclusive bonus content, get fun and funny updates on her life on the farm and more!

A Gift from Jessie

View this code through your smart phone camera to be taken to a page where you can download a FREE ebook when you sign up to get updates from Jessie Gussman! Find out why people say, "Jessie's is the only newsletter I open and read" and "You make my day brighter. Love, love, love reading your newsletters. I don't know where you find time to write books. You are so busy living life. A true blessing." and "I know from now on that I can't be drinking my morning coffee while reading your newsletter – I laughed so hard I sprayed it out all over the table!"

Claim your free book from Jessie!

Escape to more faith-filled romance series by Jessie Gussman!

The Complete Sweet Water, North Dakota Reading Order:

Series One: Sweet Water Ranch Western Cowboy Romance (11 book series)

Series Two: Coming Home to North Dakota (12 book series)

Series Three: Flyboys of Sweet Briar Ranch in North Dakota (13 book series)

Series Four: Sweet View Ranch Western Cowboy Romance (10 book series)

Spinoffs and More! Additional Series You'll Love:

Jessie's First Series: Sweet Haven Farm (4 book series)

Small-Town Romance: The Baxter Boys (5 book series)

Bad-Boy Sweet Romance: Richmond Rebels Sweet Romance (3 book series)

Sweet Water Spinoff: Cowboy Crossing (9 book series)

Small Town Romantic Comedy: Good Grief, Idaho (5 book series)

True Stories from Jessie's Farm: Stories from Jessie Gussman's Newsletter (3 book series)

Reader-Favorite! Sweet Beach Romance: Blueberry Beach (8 book series)

Blueberry Beach Spinoff: Strawberry Sands (10 book series)

From Strawberry Sands to: Raspberry Ridge (12 book series)

Swoonfully Jolly Holiday Stories:

Holiday Romance: Cowboy Mountain Christmas (6 book series)

Cowboy Mountain Christmas Spinoff: A Heartland Cowboy Christmas (9 book series)

New and Much Loved: Mistletoe Meadows (4 books and counting!)

Laughing Through the Snow: Christmas Tree, PA Sweet Romcoms (6 short reads)

Made in the USA
Middletown, DE
16 September 2025